ALWAYS THE BRIDESMAID

Never the Bride
Book 1

Emily E K Murdoch

DRAGONBLADE PUBLISHING, INC.

Dragonblade Publishing, Inc. is an imprint of Kathryn Le Veque Novels, Inc.
P.O. Box 7968
La Verne CA 91750
ceo@dragonbladepublishing.com

Produced in the United States of America

First Edition January 2020
Print Edition

ARE YOU SIGNED UP FOR DRAGONBLADE'S BLOG?

You'll get the latest news and information on exclusive giveaways, exclusive excerpts, coming releases, sales, free books, cover reveals and more.

Check out our complete list of authors, too!

No spam, no junk. That's a promise!

Sign Up Here

www.dragonbladepublishing.com

Dearest Reader;

Thank you for your support of a small press. At Dragonblade Publishing, we strive to bring you the highest quality Historical Romance from the some of the best authors in the business. Without your support, there is no 'us', so we sincerely hope you adore these stories and find some new favorite authors along the way.

Happy Reading!

CEO, Dragonblade Publishing

Additional Dragonblade books by Author Emily E K Murdoch

Never The Bride Series

Always the Bridesmaid (Book 1)

Always the Chaperone (Book 2)

Always the Courtesan (Book 3)

Always the Best Friend (Book 4)

Always the Wallflower (Book 5)

Always the Bluestocking (Book 6)

*** Please visit Dragonblade's website for a full list of books and authors. Sign up for Dragonblade's blog for sneak peeks, interviews, and more: ***

www.dragonbladepublishing.com

CHAPTER ONE

M ISS TABITHA CHESWORTH could feel her breath rising from her lungs and taste excitement and fear on her tongue as the soft morning light fell through the stained-glass windows. With one shaking hand, she smoothed the cream, silk gown embroidered with a scalloped edge. It fell to the ground like water, skimming past the dregs of snow which had lingered for two days. With her other hand, she clasped her bouquet tightly. She would not drop them, no matter how quickly her heart fluttered.

Echoes of the organ, Handel's *Water Music*, floated from the church door, and Tabitha swallowed.

"Are you ready, Miss Chesworth?"

The man's voice made her jump as the verger, an elderly man, smiled with crinkled skin around his kind eyes. His feet stomped on the stone to keep his toes warm. Her own, in her slight, leather slippers, had lost feeling.

His words seemed to come from a long way off, but she nodded. The church door opened, and Tabitha took a step forward.

It was impossible not to be overwhelmed with happiness as the heavenly sound of music rose and slow, steady steps guided her down the aisle. Tears had never been too far away from her eyes during the planning of this wedding, and she forced down the burgeoning emotions.

This was it. This was what she had been planning for, thinking about, desperate to reach for weeks now, and it hardly seemed real.

Every eye in St. Gabriel's turned toward her, and Tabitha's heart swelled...until their gazes slipped past her to the figure following her, their smiles now focused on the bride.

Tabitha's emotions turned bitter, the joy transformed into envy, so unbecoming in a woman of four and twenty. She had known her big moment in the wedding between Lieutenant Perry and her cousin, Miss Reed, would be over as soon as Mabel entered the church.

That knowledge did not remove the sting in her heart.

As she neared the end of the aisle, Tabitha tried to reason with herself. After all, to be asked to be a bridesmaid was a true honor...even if it was for the third time.

Well-practiced as she was in the art, she gave a brief smile to the nervous-looking Lieutenant and carefully stepped to the left so Mabel could meet her groom.

The young, handsome vicar had driven Bath's young ladies into such a tither, smiled out at his congregation and indicated they should be seated. Well, she had done it. After weeks of preparations, discussions, debates, and a few tears, she had managed to get Mabel to the top of the aisle.

It was wrong of her, surely *very* wrong, to feel jealousy. Tabitha shifted in her seat as shame tinged her cheeks. This was Mabel's day, not her own. Even if she wished it was.

"Dearly beloved," began Reverend Michaels, "we are gathered here today to celebrate the union between Lieutenant Thomas Perry and Miss Mabel Reed. God instituted the sanctity of marriage..."

Despite the reverend's good looks, Tabitha found it impossible to keep her mind on him or the service. It wandered, as it always did at weddings, to the other two occasions where she had been honored— and she must keep reminding herself it was an honor, for she was very grateful to be chosen as bridesmaid.

Two other cousins, both without sisters, had sent her those delightful little cards announcing their upcoming nuptials and their wish to share it with her.

A wry smile crept over Tabitha's face. She had thought, in their childhood days, that she would be the first to marry, though had never admitted it to anyone. She was the eldest, and marriage and a happy home had always been her dream. A dream of a future never to come.

Guilt washed over her, and Tabitha forced her attention back to the wedding.

"...for richer, for poorer," her cousin Mabel was saying, her hands enclasped with the young lieutenant, their eyes on each other, "in sickness and in health..."

Her mother, Tabitha's Aunt Margaret, was seated beside her. She was crying softly and sniffing something dreadful.

Tabitha rolled her eyes, but she was accustomed to wedding etiquette and well-practiced at the art of comforting mothers. She pulled a lace handkerchief from her sleeve and gently pressed it into the lady's hand.

Her aunt's blubbering halted enough for the congregation to hear the groom repeat the vows of love to his bride.

"Thank you, my dear."

Tabitha returned her smile, hopeful their interaction was over, but it was not to be.

Aunt Margaret giggled and nudged her in the ribs painfully. "Always the bridesmaid, never the bride!" Without another word, she turned back to watch her daughter become Mrs. Thomas Perry.

Tabitha's smile froze, and she forced down the anger and sadness which her aunt's thoughtless words had created.

The folklore saying had never occurred to her, but there was no denying its veracity: she had been a bridesmaid three times, three times in the last two years, and she was no closer to finding her own happily ever after.

She tried to concentrate on the prayer, but it was impossible to prevent intrusive thoughts.

She did not set high expectations for a man. If anything, her hopes were broad and easily found. Handsome if possible, of course, but there were more important qualities she had never considered in such short supply. Honesty, kindness, a strength in himself and who he was, far more important than physical prowess, and a certain disregard for the rigid rules of the *ton*...

But society, at least her society, was small. She had encountered and been introduced to almost every eligible young gentleman of her equal, as her mother would put it. Tabitha smiled bitterly at the thought. Yes, her mother had made sure of that, and not a single gentleman had caught Tabitha's attention for long.

What did one do when one's opportunities to meet eligible young gentlemen had, it seemed, come to an end? Where did she find new, potential suitors?

As delicately as she could, she tried to look around the church surreptitiously. There was Mr. Prander, Mr. McKee, and Mr. Lister. All gentlemen she had known for at least a decade, two of whom were now married. The third...well, perhaps the less said about Mr. Lister the better.

Something clenched uncomfortably in her stomach. She was not noble enough to meet any titled gentlemen, and her mother would never allow her to be introduced to a gentleman of trade.

Her gaze paused on Lieutenant Perry who was staring misty eyed at his bride. Perhaps the army was her best option. Perhaps her new cousin could introduce her to a set of gentlemen.

But would any of them be interested in courting a woman who had been a bridesmaid too many times?

Sudden movement around her jolted Tabitha from her thoughts.

"–our first hymn," Reverend Michaels was saying, and Tabitha quickly rose to join the congregation, fumbling for her hymn book.

The rich tones of the organ rose, and with them, her spirits. She was rarely despondent for long, and there was always tomorrow. There was always another chance of happiness, and who could tell? Perhaps she would meet the gentleman who was perfect for her at the next ball?

It was only when Tabitha had found the correct page of her hymnal that she realized someone was tapping her on the shoulder.

Plastering a smile on her face, she turned to see Miss Sophia Worsley, a rebellious woman well-known in Bath for her failed betrothal, with an eyebrow arched.

"Miss Chesworth," she hissed under her breath. "You simply must decide a debate between myself and Miss Seton. Is this the first or the second time you have been a bridesmaid?"

Tabitha attempted to keep her frustrated sigh quiet and widened her false smile. If she was not able to answer this question sanguinely, then the wedding reception was going to be a tortuous affair. "Actually, Miss Worsley, 'tis the third."

Miss Worsley's eyes widened, and she glanced with merriment at her friend as she whispered, "Well, you know what they say, Miss Chesworth. All you need to do to break the curse is be a bridesmaid seven times, and you are almost halfway there! Always a bridesmaid…"

"Never a bride," finished Tabitha, and she tried to laugh. It felt hollow and bitter in her throat.

The hymn started, and the congregation lifted their voices. Tabitha inclined her head politely to both Miss Worsley and Miss Seton, but before she could turn back, someone standing near the back of the church caught her attention.

It was a gentleman. He was tall with a blue, silk cravat tied most extravagantly under his neck, and he was staring at her fiercely with no shame across his face.

CHAPTER TWO

I T WAS IMPOSSIBLE for Richard St. Maur to look at the 'happy couple' without deep disdain and disgust creeping across his handsome features.

Well, it was done, and he supposed, not entirely a disaster. He had certainly attended far worse weddings than this. The woman had a solid reputation, but he never thought Perry would lower himself to matrimony in the first place.

In their college days at Oxford, they had joked about such men: swains to love, utter slaves to the whims of another, without any thought or care for themselves.

And yet, here Perry was. Debased to the stooping lows of marriage, chained forever to a woman, doomed to repeat the mistakes of all those before him.

An irritated cough he recognized disturbed his thoughts, and Richard turned to his sister, Charlotte, who looked pointedly at her hymn book. Richard rolled his eyes, picked up his own book, and rustled through the delicate pages.

A beam of light pierced his dark brown eyes, and Richard screwed them up, shifting in the pew away from the light. It must have been two years since he stepped inside a church. But then, it had been three years since he had vowed never to marry. The line of the Dukes of Axwickes will end with him.

My God, three years. Richard felt the exhaustion in his bones. Yet, it had been the right decision, he was still sure of that. After everything his father had done, or not done, it was hardly a difficult choice that the male line must end.

His father had been an only child, and there was only Charlotte and himself left. It was a strange thing to consider, the end of the St. Maur line, and him the last, but it was the right decision. No more could ever come after him.

The name of Axwick would go to the Winslows, those distant cousins he had never met, and much good it would do them.

He had never been tempted to rescind that promise, no matter how many ladies in tight corsets had fluttered by him at the races, or at Almack's, or crossed the street before him in tantalizing bonnets, kicking up their skirts with shrieks of mock horror.

But no. 'Twas not for him, the entrapment of matrimony and the continuation of the family line. The world had enough drunkards and gamblers without adding any more.

The singing had begun, and Richard opened his mouth to join them when a casual glance over the top of his hymnal made him stop, mouth open.

One of the bridesmaids was speaking to a pair of young ladies behind her—*chittering about the cost of the silk gown, no doubt*—and in all other occasions, he would have ignored them.

But she was different. Something hot in his stomach lurched, and he craned his neck to see more of her.

It was unfathomable that such a woman was a bridesmaid and not the bride. To his astonishment, she was a rare thing indeed: a true beauty.

He realized his mouth was still open, and he shut it quickly, feeling the tension of embarrassment in his shoulders.

How could this be? It was bizarre to have such a strong reaction to her—a woman that he had never even met before. A score of people separated them in the church, but there was something...a spark, an attraction, call it what you will, but it had grabbed hold of his stomach and twisted it in a knot.

Her eyes lifted from her conversation and met his own.

Richard gasped under his breath, a low sound none heard but himself. Her eyes, green and sparkling, had more presence in them than diamonds glittering in candlelight.

He must speak with her. He could not fathom where the need came from and had never felt a need like it.

A delicate pink touched her cheeks, and the woman turned back to face the front of the church, her hymnal raised.

Richard luxuriated in his power. He was no fool; if his title was not enough to turn the heads of most pretty young things, his height, charming smile, and serious countenance usually did the rest.

So, she had noticed him, too. All the better. Richard stretched his shoulders and grinned. Just because he had vowed off marriage didn't mean he was completely forbidden from worldly pleasures, after all. It was not a hardship to imagine losing oneself in the arms of a woman that was startlingly beautiful.

By God, he would love nothing more than to pull her closer than appropriate so she could feel the scandalous nature of their embrace, and then closer still so their lips…

"Why aren't you singing?" Charlotte's whisper was accompanied by a nudge to his ribs, and Richard nudged her back instinctively.

He swallowed. Well, he would not lose anything by asking, would he?

"Who is the pretty bridesmaid?"

Charlotte glanced at him, an eyebrow raised.

"That one." He nodded at the woman who had turned away so prettily.

"The one with the chestnut-colored hair?"

Richard smiled. He was immediately thumped on the arm by his sister.

"You are not to go mistress hunting in *church*," Charlotte whispered, half scandalized, half laughing. "Can you do nothing to control yourself, Richard, or must I warn every woman I meet against you?"

"Please do," he whispered back. "You will only direct them to me, with that sort of introduction. Have you not learned young ladies want what is dangerous and forbidden?"

He did not need to glance at Charlotte to know she was rolling her eyes. His older sister had always been the more sensible of the two of them, but not bearing the weight of the line of Axwickes helped. It was a terrible thing to be the heir.

His gaze remained on the bridesmaid. She appeared to be singing most studiously, but Richard had been seducing women for years now. He knew that slightly uncomfortable look, the delicate way she held herself perfectly still so as not to attract attention.

Prey frozen in the gaze of its predator.

"And her name?"

Charlotte murmured, "Miss Tabitha Chesworth, if you must know."

Just hearing her name sent a chill down Richard's spine. What power did this strange woman hold over him that he'd be captivated from just one look?

"Miss Tabitha Chesworth," he repeated.

"Shh!"

The St. Maur siblings turned to stare at the elderly woman who had so violently shushed them from her pew, he in surprise that anyone should shush him, and Charlotte in embarrassment.

"I am sorry, madam," she rushed in a *sotto voce* voice. "I—"

"Shh!" The elderly woman brought a finger to her lips this time, and Richard chuckled as he turned his mortified and blushing sister around.

Miss Chesworth was still stoically facing forward, and Richard grinned. Yes, he may be utterly captivated by her, but it appeared the interest was entirely mutual.

It would not be too difficult for him to speak with Miss Chesworth, together with Charlotte at first, and then alone at the reception for the happy couple. Conversation would be light in general, even vague, then specific, intimate, and personal. How difficult would it be to tempt her away to a more secluded place to continue that conversation?

A conversation that would hardly need words at that point, though Richard's tongue could still do all the talking. A chance to…get to know each other better.

A sharp dig in the ribs made him cry out. "Ouch, Charlotte, that hurt!"

"Shh!"

"No, Richard, I forbid it," Charlotte whispered fiercely this time, completely ignoring the old woman behind them who found their conversation so offensive.

Richard raised an eyebrow. "You do not even know what I am planning yet!"

His sister raised an eyebrow in turn, and he smiled wickedly.

"Well, perhaps you do," he admitted in a low voice, "but I have not even asked to be introduced yet. You could not have possibly guessed I would ask that favor of you."

Charlotte glared. "Richard, I know you far too well. Miss Chesworth is undoubtedly seeking marriage, not a sordid liaison."

Richard licked his lips. It was impossible not to undress Miss Tabitha Chesworth with his mind, now that he knew her name. The gentle folds of her gown brushed what promised to be a delightful curve of the hips, and her waist…

"I mean it, Richard," his sister warned. "She will want to be wedded not bedded."

But her words were easy to ignore. "I will not be traipsed down the aisle by a young miss looking to add a title to her name, but I will have Miss Tabitha Chesworth for my own."

"Be quiet, sir! Who do you think you are?"

Richard was not accustomed to being ordered about, and after the third time, his always short temper finally burst.

Turning around and drawing himself up to his not inconsiderable height, he glared at the elderly woman with a look of righteous judgement and affixed her with his most impressive, nobleman's glare.

"I am St. Maur, the sixteenth Duke of Axwick, and this is my sister, Lady Charlotte," Richard hissed in a whisper that nonetheless carried the length and breadth of the church, "and if I wish to speak with her, then I will!"

Not for the first time in his life, scandalized gasps echoed around him as the organ finished its last note.

The congregation and the St. Maur siblings with them, sat.

"You cannot just take what you want all of the time," Charlotte said close to his ear, cheeks flushed with embarrassment.

Richard was barely listening. His eyes had remained on Miss Chesworth, and they were not disappointed. She turned, and her blush crept delightfully toward her breasts.

Something in his throat growled. "Yes, I can."

CHAPTER THREE

"...a ND YOU MUST be absolutely thrilled!"

"Yes, how proud you must be!"

"I mean, to be asked once is such an honor, but to be asked to be a bridesmaid for the third time…"

Tabitha's face ached from the false smile she'd held for the last half an hour. A cluck of old biddies had surrounded her as soon as they had entered the home of Lieutenant Perry's father, telling her just how fortunate she should consider herself to have walked down the aisle multiple times.

She blinked. There had been a lull in the noise, and the three elderly ladies were staring at her expectantly.

Tabitha nodded graciously. "'Tis indeed a remarkable honor."

The ladies relaxed, and one of them nodded. "Ah, yes, such an honor. And it says so much about you, too, dear."

With that, they wandered off.

"It does indeed," Tabitha breathed, the false smile cracking at the corners. "It says I am useful, never considered for marriage itself, but a rather nice part of the decorations."

It was impossible to ignore the boiling of her blood. Would she always be a pleasant part of the day but never the reason for it? How many more weddings would she endure? Even if she was never a bridesmaid again, she would be forevermore the eternal bridesmaid.

"Are you feeling quite well, Tabitha?"

The innocent question forced her back to her senses, and it was a natural smile as she stretched her hands to the bride.

"I could not be happier," she lied, and the new Mrs. Perry beamed at her.

"It truly has been a wonderful day, has it not?" her cousin breathed, smiling at the throng of well-wishers who were evidently waiting respectfully for her to finish their conversation before rushing forward to give her their felicitations. "I could not even dream Lady Romeril would attend, but we sent an invitation out of courtesy, and I am beyond grateful we did. And the flowers in the church, so elegantly arranged, I would not have thought it within Mrs. Howarth's powers to…"

Tabitha allowed the happiness to wash over her and squeezed her cousin's hand gently. It was not Mabel's fault. To be passed over for marriage at her age, a cruel four and twenty… But there it was. Perhaps it was not so old, but most of her peers were confined with their second child. Every year fresh young ladies came out for their first season, prettier and more accomplished than every season before them.

"My love, come and enjoy the festivities!" Lieutenant Perry rushed into the room to draw his bride to his side. "Major Bowden is at the pianoforte and is threatening to sing a duet with my mother!"

His voice matched his jovial spirit, and Tabitha smiled as her cousin scampered away with a laugh, hand in hand with her husband.

Her heart ached. What wouldn't she give for someone she loved to look at her like that and seek her out in a crowded room? For a man to pause and wait for her because nothing else mattered but to hear her opinion.

Fires filled every grate in the room, and candles added to the heat haze around the walls. Everyone of note in Bath had been invited to the Perry wedding, and plenty had deemed it worthy enough to descend from London, too.

Tabitha sighed. There was not a single person who she would love to talk to, to hear laugh, to jest with. There was no one seeking her out, desperate for her opinion on the latest play, or interested to hear her thoughts on the latest scandalous activity of Lord Byron.

"Champagne?"

Tabitha jumped as a servant appeared at her side, offering a flute of champagne—a real treat with the troubles in France. Uncle Reed must have broken the bank for his daughter's nuptials.

"Thank you," she said mechanically, taking one from the silver platter offered to her. Everyone had come together here today to celebrate the wedding—as they should be—and all she was doing was standing, feeling bitter and selfish.

"Miss Chesworth? Miss Tabitha Chesworth?"

A voice had called out her name, a voice she did not recognize. Tabitha turned her head to see a woman walking toward her with an anxious smile. She was tall, had probably once been quite beautiful, but was past the bloom of youth and was walking arm in arm with a gentleman that was not.

He was the most handsome and striking man she had ever seen. Tall, dark, with a jaw that could cut ice, and fierce eyes staring at her as though she were a fox in a hunt.

Tabitha felt her cheeks flush. It was the gentleman from the church, the one near the back who had watched her so carefully.

Heat blossomed from her heart, and she was glad of the cold champagne glass cooling her as the couple approached, recognizing the lady as a friend of her cousin's. What could she possibly want with her?

They reached her, and the lady inclined her head in the respectable courtesies expected of polite society. Tabitha followed suit but could not help noticing the gentleman did not take his eyes from her, nor did he bow.

The room was too hot, and her corset had been tied too tightly that morning.

"We met last week at Mabel's—Mrs. Perry's, I mean—home as she prepared for today," the lady was saying to her. "Lady Charlotte St. Maur. What a truly wonderful wedding it was."

Tabitha swallowed, her throat dry and eyes drawn to the silent gentleman beside Lady Charlotte. Her brother? Her betrothed? "Yes, yes it was."

Hardly aware what she was agreeing to, hardly comprehending what was happening in the rest of the room, her eyes could not leave the gentleman who had, as yet, said nothing. His gaze still had not left hers, and she felt the presence of him.

Lady Charlotte nodded. "May I have the pleasure of introducing you to my brother, Miss Chesworth?" Without waiting for a response, as though she had decided Tabitha was to meet him and there was nothing else for it. "Miss Chesworth, Richard St. Maur, sixteenth Duke of Axwick."

Now the gentleman bowed, but what a bow: short, sharp, as though he had rarely been forced to bow to anyone in his life. Tabitha was so stunned by his attractive countenance, she completely forgot to curtsy.

"You look very beautiful, Miss Chesworth." His voice was deep, dark even, more serious than any other.

Tabitha wished she had not been close to the fire when they had advanced on her, for it felt like an attack, this barrage of brother and sister.

"Thank you, your grace," she managed to say quietly, heart fluttering and hands clasped around the stem of the champagne glass rather than drift awkwardly at her sides.

The Duke chuckled, his eyes not wavering from her. "Now then, I do not hold with such niceties created by pompous old ladies and gentlemen who never actually meet each other. I would much prefer it if you called me Richard."

It was all Tabitha could do to prevent her jaw from dropping at this *risqué* way of speaking, and they had only just met! But there was a warmth to the Duke of Axwick that none could ignore, and she smiled despite herself.

"And I would prefer it," she said, her smile unwavering under the intensity of his own, "if I called you Axwick."

"Perhaps we can compromise," the duke countered, his lip curling. "May I be St. Maur?"

Tabitha laughed. Well, he was charming, and she could not deny it was pleasant to exchange witticisms with a man so handsome, drawing so many admiring looks from other ladies.

Lady Charlotte was staring first at her and then at her brother, surprise on her face.

Tabitha swallowed. She was not going to be beaten by this man, even if he was the sixteenth of his line. She may just be Miss Tabitha Chesworth, but she could take on a duke.

"You would prefer St. Maur?" she asked sweetly. "Axwick it is, then."

The duke threw back his head and laughed, and it was his first genuine laugh that she had heard. It was rich like brandy butter, smooth and delicious, and one that sparked something hot that had nothing to do with the fire behind her.

"Lady Charlotte!"

A young lady in a light blue gown and drenched in diamonds poked her head around a doorframe and was gesturing wildly to their group by the fire. "Lady Charlotte, may we borrow you?"

Tabitha saw a flicker of annoyance pass over Lady Charlotte's face before she adjusted her features.

"You must excuse me," she said, curtseying low.

Tabitha barely had time to return the curtsy before she realized she was alone with the Duke of Axwick. The crowded room had been forgotten, and Charlotte had felt like their chaperone, as for all intents and purposes, but now they were alone by the fire.

Panic rose in her throat and dried out her mouth. The duke was such a *man*, he was more man than anyone she had ever met, and she was standing with him. His very presence reminded her she was naught but a gentlewoman, and he one of the nobility of England and Ireland.

People like them simply did not mix. A duke and a Chesworth? Her father would have laughed to even think it, and he had been a most mild-mannered man.

And yet…there was something warming about *Richard's* company. She must not falter and start to adopt signs of familiarity. Where would that lead?

"You are not easily convinced, then," he said with a shake of his head. "Ah, Miss Chesworth, I wish you could call me Richard. Then I, you see, could call you Tabitha."

The way his tongue caressed her name made her overwhelmingly hot. Typically, flirtation only happened between members of the same class. Dukes did not decide to say such things to her!

But she managed to smile. "I have always known my own mind on things, and I see no reason to compromise now."

"What is on your mind at this wedding?" The duke stretched out his hands to indicate the merriment.

"It was a lovely day with a beautiful bride. We could not have hoped for better weather."

She had expected him to jump at the mediocre topic, a casual and, most importantly, neutral topic that could see them through until his sister, Lady Charlotte, returned.

He chuckled, throwing his head back again. "My dear, Miss Chesworth, your reply is so perfect that it is practically rehearsed!" He took a step forward, closing the gap between them. "Now, tell me. What do you really think?"

She hesitated. There was something about him, duke or no, that confused her. His eyes went through her, right to the core of who she really was, not who she would like to be. There was a fierce intelligence in his eyes, eyes directed firmly at her.

No, she was all he was interested in, and it frightened her as much as it thrilled her.

"It is my true opinion," she began, but he interrupted her.

"Do not lie to me, Miss Chesworth." His voice was so low she could barely catch it over the rabble of the revelry, and he took another step forward. They were standing so close now that if she wanted to, she could have allowed her right hand to fall to her side and it would have brushed his own. "You do not need to hide anything from me. We need not have secrets from each other, we barely know each other."

"And that is precisely why I shall not pour my heart out to you," Tabitha managed to counter in a friendly voice, her heart fluttering.

He shrugged. "Such things have never stopped me."

Tabitha laughed at what she presumed to be a jest and took a sip of her champagne. The bubbles tickled her nose as she took a large mouthful, but the bubbles and alcohol were nothing to the giddiness that Richard, Duke of Axwick, was creating.

"You do not believe me." His words were not accusatory, merely factual.

She shook her head. "I think you tease me, your grace."

His smile was broad as he replied, "Most likely. I tease my sister, Charlotte, something terrible. But you are not like her, I think."

She will be mistress of herself. She will not allow this gentleman's charming words to overwhelm her. "You think so?"

How was it possible that this man had sought her out? Tabitha took a steadying breath.

"I know so." The duke's gaze had not left her face. "I have always considered myself a just judge of character, and I believe I have all I need to distinguish your characteristics."

Tabitha laughed. "My, you speak very decidedly. After five minutes of conversation, you believe you have worked me out?"

"Certainly. You are proud, but careful not to show it. Proud of your family, your beliefs. That is something you have worked hard on, and yet it means that few people see the real Miss Tabitha Chesworth underneath all the layers of decorum and control."

Her mouth fell open. The duke's brown eyes were bright, but not mischievous. He was smiling, but not joking.

How did he know all that? As though he had looked into her very soul?

"I am sure you say that to all young ladies you seek to flatter," she said airily.

"Perhaps. Perhaps not. Maybe I am the first gentleman to see you precisely for who you are."

The room was not exactly spinning, but Tabitha's feet were unsteady.

"And yet I know very little about you," she managed to say.

"True, but I am sure you can guess. Try me."

The duke spread his hands out wide to give her full view of him and waited for her to speak.

Tabitha swallowed. This was not how she had expected their conversation to develop, and now she was being asked to speak to a gentleman's character—a duke's! This was not the time to step away fearfully. What did she have to lose?

"You, sir, like to tease everyone," she said, a little shocked at her own daring. The duke's eyebrows raised as she continued, "You mock because it is better than serious conversation. With serious conversation, you would be forced to give your true opinion, and then you could be held to it. Far easier to never give one."

She held her breath as the words sunk in, but despite her brazen observations, he smiled.

"Well said, Miss Chesworth. You are not like the other young ladies I have encountered, but then, three times the bridesmaid, you must have unending wisdom."

Pain shot through her stomach like a knife. Just as their flirtation was gaining pace, he had to throw those words in her face. But then, the Duke of Axwick did not appear to realize his sentence had pained her. He was still looking at her with an appreciative look, his gaze taking in more than just her face.

"And you are clearly without wisdom at all," she managed to say lightly. "But then, I suppose you have little to share."

Had she gone too far? No, he laughed, and his appraising look now appeared a little surprised to hear her defend herself so astutely.

"You and Charlotte would agree on that point, I think," he said good naturedly. "But I like to think I have a little sense. I am the gentleman, after all, that sought you out."

Tabitha's breath caught in her throat. His voice was serious.

"One of the better decisions of today." The duke grinned. "I do not think I can give Lieutenant Perry the same praise."

They were very much alone now. For some reason, they were being given a wide berth by the other wedding guests, though plenty of glances were being shot their way. Tabitha could not think why, but her mind was entirely occupied with attempting to keep up with the duke's conversation.

"The lieutenant has done something to offend you?"

A dark shadow crossed over the Duke of Axwick's face. "He has married, 'tis all, and there are few who would critique him for it, but I would not have advised it."

A flicker of concern bloomed in Tabitha's heart. A duke would never consider her for marriage, that would be ridiculous—but a small part of her, until that moment, had hoped.

"You think marriage is not advisable?" she managed to ask calmly.

He frowned. "Marriage of any kind is to be avoided, but a gentleman in Perry's position, to be called to war at any time, never knowing what the next year will hold... 'Tis not a life for a woman."

Tabitha's face relaxed into a relieved smile. "So, you do not prescribe against marriage in general."

"Ah, I must disagree with you there," the duke said quietly. "Here, I will prove it to you. I will tell you something I have only ever told one other person in the world. I am never going to get married."

Instead of impressing her, as he clearly intended to, Tabitha felt a surge of instant disappointment—and was forced to scold herself silently. *What would a duke want with me?* She had no connections, no cousins who were earls, or great aunts or uncles with honorifics after their name.

This was casual flirting, of course.

"Not going to be married?" Tabitha arched an eyebrow and allowed her right arm to fall to her side. "And have you made this decision based on the scarcity of eligible young ladies?"

"Nay, Miss Chesworth, there are plenty. Indeed, a very beautiful one is standing right before me."

Tabitha's body grew warmer, but her curiosity got the better of her, and instead of coquettishly playing along with him, she asked the question actually on her mind. "Why then?"

"Ah." The duke smiled broadly. "That would be telling."

"Yes, it would," said Tabitha without thinking, taking a step closer. Her hand grazed his.

She was consumed by the sensation of him. Her champagne flute still clutched in her hand was now pressed between his waistcoat and her silk gown.

Their eyes met with such intensity that Tabitha gasped. Something strange was happening.

"Miss Tabitha Chesworth," murmured the Duke of Axwick in a low voice only she could hear, "I would very much like to get to know you better."

"Well then," she whispered, losing all sense of propriety, all sense of where they were, and just speaking from the desire flaming through her heart, "there is no time like the present."

The duke opened his mouth, and Tabitha's heart skipped a beat, so thrilled was she to be saying these words. It was madness to be standing close to a man who had this effect on her, an effect she barely understood but wanted, but before he could say a word...

"Miss Chesworth? It is you I spied hiding away there near the fire!"

"Is it the missing bridesmaid? Thank goodness, we can make a full reel!"

The duke breathed out with a shaky laugh. "I might have said something rather wild there."

Tabitha took a step back. The distance between them was empty and cold now, and she regretted it, hating whoever it was who was calling her away from this mysterious and delectable man. "And I might have listened to you. But duty calls, Axwick."

He nodded, and without saying another word, she walked away from him.

It was a wonder she was able to walk at all, and when she thought about it later that evening, toasty and curled up under the bedclothes at home, with the heat of a warming pan defrosting her toes, she wondered how she didn't fall over, so intoxicated was she with the duke's presence.

She had not turned around as she had walked away from him. She had not needed to. She had felt his stare watching her every step.

CHAPTER FOUR

"**G**OD IN HEAVEN!" Richard's curse was low, unintended for anyone else, not that it would have mattered. He had been alone for hours.

This was the last thing he needed, to open another box and find a mass of bills. He had been convinced the box cleared the day before was the last, but no. They kept arriving at Number Fourteen, Queen Square, Bath.

Even in the dim evening light, he could make out the name Arnold in a fine ink script, always paired with numbers: fifty guineas, one hundred pounds, four thousand guineas...

Richard leaned back in the peeling, leather armchair in his study. He should have listened to his instincts. It had been too good to be true when his butler, Matthews, had said it was the last of them. It was enticing, the thought that he had finally dealt with all his brother's debts.

The fifteenth duke had had few friends but plenty of enemies. Renown for being loose with his cash, loose with his morals, and terrible at cards, he had been sought out and robbed over and over again.

Richard would have had sympathy for him if the fool hadn't enjoyed it so much.

And now his brother's club had sent a servant, and low and behold, Arnold had stashed another three boxes of debts there.

It was their father all over again. A candle guttered on the mantle-piece as Richard rubbed his tired, aching eyes. This was a painful and rather raw reminder of the pressure he had endured when he had been forced to go through his father's debts three years ago.

The fourteenth duke had passed on his vices to his eldest son, while Richard, the younger and therefore ignored, had watched them drink and gamble the family wealth away.

When their father had died, it was Richard's responsibility to try to untangle just how much the family coffers owed, while his good-for-nothing brother, Arnold, had done nothing about it—nothing but increase his own gambling stakes.

He was the duke by then, after all, not the heir apparent.

The study door opened, and without glancing up, Richard barked, "What now?"

There was a dignified silence. Richard looked up through untidy hair and saw Matthews in the doorway, apologetic...and holding an ominous, mahogany box in his hands.

"My apologies for interrupting you, your grace," the butler said stiffly, "but this box has been delivered ...by a bookmaker from the East End."

"By the devil's teeth," cursed Richard, not bothering to keep it under his breath this time, head dropping to his hands. "Thank you, Matthews. Just add it to the pile, will you? I doubt I will complete it today, but best to have it all together."

The butler obeyed, and without another word, exited the study, closing the door quietly behind him.

Richard muttered aloud to the empty room, "When will I ever be finished paying off these damned mistakes of the Axwickes?"

"As long as you do not make any new mistakes of your own, very soon."

Richard jumped to his feet as his sister Charlotte rose from a high-backed chair drawn close to the fire.

She was holding a book and smiling. "I do not recommend Mrs. Radcliffe if you scare so easily, Richard," she said in a serious voice. "'Tis not for the faint of heart, her novels."

Sinking back into his chair, Richard asked dryly, "And have you been enjoying the perils of Mrs. Radcliffe all evening, Charlotte?"

His sister moved gracefully around the boxes on the floor to sit opposite him at the rather grand desk—so grand, thought Richard, that perhaps they should have sold it.

"You returned from Lieutenant Perry's wedding in an utterly foul mood," she said starkly. "And you have not shaken yourself out of it since."

Richard frowned. "Arnold left us in such a hole that 'tis taking all my energy to pull us out of it."

Before he could stop her, Charlotte leaned forward and picked up one of the debts. "Can I help?"

Richard snatched it from her, incensed, embarrassment flooding through him at the idea that a woman—his sister!—would belittle herself with such matters. "This is my burden to bear, Charlotte, leave well alone. You are utterly useless in this matter and without a dowry, you are permanently stuck with me!"

The hastily spoken words rang out into the silent room. Charlotte's hand was still outstretched, but her gaze had not left him. They were wide, full of horror, and brimming with tears.

In a rustle of skirts, she rose to leave the room, but Richard, cursing himself silently for his temper, reached out. "I apologize," he said gruffly. "I did not... I have no wish to be cruel to you, Lotty. 'Tis just..."

Words appeared to fail him, and Charlotte glared with a sharpness he recognized: the Axwick fury.

He tried to quell the anger, the bitterness, the hurt that she thought he could not do it on his own and forced a smile.

"I am over-worn with guilt," he said. "It consumes me, causing me to say things I have no right to—which are not true. I am sorry the Axwick estate has naught to give you, though you need nothing to tempt a gentleman to offer for your hand."

He thought she would leave him in a temper and rightly so, but Charlotte said nothing as she lowered herself gently back into the chair. The tears did not fall, but Richard could not pretend there wasn't hurt still in her features.

She spoke in a barely controlled voice, "I make a much better chaperone anyway."

Richard felt his stomach contract painfully as he saw the bitter truth in his sister's face. She was over thirty now and was invited to balls as a chaperone rather than as a dance partner—not that he would ever admit it to her face. Wild horses could not have dragged it from him.

"Nonsense," he said gruffly. "Any man wise enough to see your beauty and your worth, Charlotte, will have an easy conversation with me. I swear it."

She did laugh this time. "I am not sure whether a gentleman should ask you permission, Richard, you are so abrupt! And after all, all this concern may not be necessary. I could end up with a very nice dowry, if you were only to marry well!"

Her laughter did nothing to lighten his mood.

"You know full well," Richard said a little more tersely than he had intended, "I have vowed never to marry. The line ends with me."

"But Richard–"

"No," he cut across her. "No, Lotty. The Axwickes have proved again and again to have tainted blood in the male line, weak blood, weak men. I will never wed, and the Axwick line will end with me."

He had expected her to be solemn at his words and try to dissuade him as she had always tried.

But she laughed. "You were rather taken with Miss Tabitha Chesworth today."

Richard stiffened. Miss Tabitha Chesworth had been forgotten when he entered the study four hours ago, determined on naught but the task ahead. But as soon as Charlotte mentioned her name, he was transported back.

By God, she was beautiful. They had stood together for some minutes, alone in a sea of people. He had moved closer to her, that delectable body, and she had not moved away—she had moved toward him, and he had felt the quickening of her heart.

She had not known her power over him, and he had seen the desire in her eyes. The way her eyes had flickered across his features, the curve of her smile as she suggested those delightful words...

"Well then, there is no time like the present."

It was indulgent to lose oneself in tantalizing memories, but Richard was rudely awakened by laughter.

Richard scowled at her good naturedly. "'Tis no crime to allow one's thoughts to dwell on a pretty woman."

"No crime at all," Charlotte countered sweetly, "unless of course, one has taken a vow never to marry."

"That does not preclude...other things."

His sister rolled her eyes. They had always been open with each other as children, and that had continued into adulthood. He hardly paraded his paramours before her, but Charlotte was under no illusion he found comfort in the arms of the beautiful and the...available...from time to time.

"Well, do not waste your time on her."

Richard frowned, strangely eager to prove his charm suitable to bring down Miss Tabitha Chesworth's gown around her ankles. "Why the devil not?"

Charlotte frowned. "Because I asked her cousin, the bride, and she told me Tabitha was quite open with her acquaintances about her desire to marry. To *marry,* Richard. Not be seduced."

Richard smiled thoughtfully. Well, he had never been turned

down before, and even the thought he could be refused was a rather thrilling one.

But only one or two of his previous conquests had been purchased with jewels or coin. The rest had been bought with flattery, and if there was one thing he was sure of, his tongue was more than enough of a tool to get women warm for him.

"I see no reason why I could not succeed," he said aloud. "She is hardly a nun, is she, this Miss Chesworth?"

His sister shook her head. "No, but the rules of propriety are not ones easily set aside."

Ah, the challenge. Richard shifted in his seat, the mere thought of wooing Tabitha causing him to get stiff. All women were essentially the same, after all. How hard could it be?

He said with a nonchalant air, "Charlotte, have you responded to the invitation to a ball from Lady Romeril?"

"Why?" she asked suspiciously.

Richard grinned. "I have a favor to ask—a new friend of yours to add to the guest list."

CHAPTER FIVE

I T WAS IMPOSSIBLE not to be mesmerized by the swirling colors as a line of couples moved delicately, intersecting and weaving as they danced the *La Royale*.

Lady Romeril's ball was not one to miss. Held each season in Bath, only the best people were invited. As Tabitha sipped from a silver goblet—Lady Romeril never missed the opportunity to show off—she marveled at the fact she had been invited at all.

There was a heady scent of lavender, punch, and people in the air. She was standing feet from the musicians, and she admired the way the candles flickered at the speed in which they played.

"—and of course, I had to accept."

Tabitha started at Lady Romeril's words and attempted to hide the fact she had not been listening. "You do not say, my lady? I had always thought—"

"I do indeed," Lady Romeril said with a pompous nod of the head. "And at great personal expense, mark you—but then, anything the darling Regent asks of me, how could I refuse?"

The ability to nod infrequently and appear to be listening carefully was all that was needed. No one wished to hear her opinion. They just wanted to share their own.

She felt a gentle nudge, and Tabitha smiled at her friend Letitia Cavendish who had the misfortune of being with her when Lady Romeril had descended. As their host continued chattering, Tabitha's eyes widened at Letitia, who stifled a laugh.

"...and so, Lieutenant Perry thought, when he delivered my wedding invitation *personally*..." Lady Romeril said impressively, turning her gaze back to her younger listeners and smiling regally. "It was awfully kind of him to deliver it himself, but then I was the guest of honor, you see—"

"Except for the bride, of course." Tabitha bit her lip as soon as the words were out of her mouth. What had possessed her to say such a thing—and to Lady Romeril, too, one of the matriarchs of Bath society?

Letitia had flushed with embarrassment on her behalf, but as Tabitha had suspected, Lady Romeril was paying her no attention.

"Yes, a very beautiful wedding," she mused. "Few brides could have compared to me on my wedding day, but I do think Miss Mabel could be one of them. You were there, were you not, Lady Letitia?"

Letitia's flush had only just begun to subside when she was called upon to make actual conversation with her hostess, and when she spoke it was with a splutter.

"W-Why yes, madam. I was honored to be invited."

Lady Romeril beamed. "Did you not think..."

Although it was most impolite to allow her mind to wander, Tabitha could not help it. The room was hot, Lady Romeril most tiresome, and there was so much to look at.

Her gaze drifted back to the dancing couples. It was a different set, and one immediately caught her eye. Wearing a brilliant, scarlet gown was Miss Emma Tilbury, the mistress of the Earl of Marnmouth.

Tabitha stared at her, her dark cascading hair, haughty eyes, and the casual disdain for the rules of society. Miss Tilbury was dancing wildly, throwing her hands in the air and moving so quickly, her skirts flashed glimpses not just of her ankles, but her knees.

Tabitha lowered her gaze in embarrassment. Just the thought of being a gossiped-about mistress and invited to an occasion such as this,

He laughed with her, and something painful stirred in her stomach. She would not allow herself to hope. He had been direct with her; she knew he was not looking for a bride.

But if one's person was flattered, was there any harm?

"I did not know you were acquainted with our Regent."

"I am not," she confessed, "but I read the newspapers like anyone else, and though I believe most of it to be false, some truth must be reported occasionally, even if it is by accident."

"You have strong opinions for one so young," Axwick observed as the dancers came to the end of their set behind him.

Tabitha flushed. "Not so young as I once was."

"Who is?" He shrugged. "But you have evidently put your time to good use, Miss Chesworth. I will admit, I enjoy conversing with you. And that is more than I can say for most of the chittering ladies in here."

A moment of understanding flitted between them, and heat rose in her chest.

Flirtations she had had with a few gentleman, but nothing had emerged of any seriousness. This was different. She knew it could amount to nothing, but somehow that made it more wild, more adventurous. She could say anything to the Duke of Axwick and not lose him. She did not have him. She never could.

Letitia nudged her.

"Have you had the pleasure of being introduced to Lady Letitia Cavendish?" Tabitha asked, turning to smile at her friend.

Letitia, never comfortable with new people at the best of times, stared back with equal panic, but her elegant breeding came to the fore. She smiled at Axwick nervously.

Axwick gave her friend a perfunctory bow.

"Lady Letitia, Richard St. Maur, sixteenth Duke of Axwick," Tabitha said.

A feeling crept into her heart never felt before, and it was fear, fear that Axwick would take one look at Letitia, a beauty and a Cavendish, and forget her.

The musicians still played, the dancers still danced, a horde of guests were circulating the room, chatting, laughing, scolding, but they all fell away silently into the background when he was standing before her. *Do not forget me.*

"And are you enjoying Lady Romeril's ball, Lady Letitia?"

His question was innocuous, but Letitia's face turned beetroot red as she stammered incoherently.

Tabitha moved quickly to rescue her friend. "We have both greatly enjoyed the evening so far. Lady Romeril's entertainment is always first rate."

She glanced at Letitia. Nature was cruel to give her such beauty and shyness.

"I do not believe I had the pleasure of seeing you at one of Lady Romeril's previous balls," the duke continued, seemingly oblivious to the sharp embarrassment he was causing in one young lady, and the fire of envy in the other. "Are you often in Bath, Lady Letitia?"

Letitia turned her gaze pleadingly toward Tabitha.

"We both come for the Season," Tabitha said, more than a little pleased to have his attention. "Lady Letitia and I have been intimate acquaintances due to a happy accident a few years ago. A gown of mine was delivered to her. The ensuing confusion enabled us to grow close, and we enjoy our time in Bath prodigiously."

She watched the duke's gaze move up and down Letitia's form and felt an overwhelming desire to step in front of her friend and block her from his view. This was madness; she barely knew him, and yet she felt so possessive over him as though he was her husband.

Her husband. What a wild thought—it shocked her to think of such a thing. He was not in the matrimony market.

Another dance suddenly ended, and the musicians received their well-earned applause. Tabitha clapped, but when she turned back to

Axwick, he was still staring at her.

"Would you like to dance, Miss Chesworth?"

His gaze was hungry.

The musicians began their opening notes of the next dance, and gentlemen reached for the hands of ladies.

Tabitha tried to breathe. "Dance?"

Axwick smiled, and the handsome lines of his face only became more pronounced. "'Tis customary when one attends a ball to seek out the most beautiful woman in the room and elicit her permission to dance. You know me, Miss Chesworth. Ever a slave to decorum."

A prickle of delight crept over Tabitha, and she could not help but smile. It would be a mistake to become more intimately acquainted with a man who had told her that his intentions were certainly not marital. The very last thing she should do is entertain a connection to such a man.

He was a gentleman who not only knew what he wanted but was determined to get it. Tabitha flushed at the suggestion.

Her.

The gentle refusal was already forming in her mind—careful, considerate, and best of all, certain—but it got lost on the way to her tongue. There was something about this man, something that drew her to him, something she could not resist. Did not want to resist.

"Thank you, Axwick," she said lightly, as though she had not been forced to conquer an internal struggle to accept him. She held out a hand.

Letitia's eyes and mouth were open, and Tabitha knew precisely why. To speak to a duke in such an intimate manner! To call him by his title, in complete disregard for society's rules...and in public.

It was hard for Tabitha to remember that this was only their second meeting.

As intoxicating as the duke was, Tabitha was not totally insensitive of Letitia's disappointment. She was to lose her companion by the wall, and Tabitha's heart broke for her. In a family like the Cavendishes, one did not breed a wallflower.

Concerns for her friend selfishly slipped away as Axwick took her hand and placed it on his arm, causing pleasant shivers up and down her spine.

With each step they took, Tabitha felt more and more people staring, and by the time they reached the end of the set, it felt as though the weight of the world was upon them.

Perhaps it was her imagination, but there were a few whispers and glances of surprise at the striking but aloof Duke of Axwick taking to the dance floor. A lady pointed at her, raising her eyebrows in surprise.

Axwick murmured, "Are you ready to call me St. Maur yet?"

Tabitha smiled as he took his place in the set. "As I have still only spent a total of fifteen minutes in your company, I cannot help but feel Axwick is more appropriate."

The musicians struck up their introductory notes, and Tabitha dipped into a curtsey along with the other women standing in a row to her right.

"Will thirty minutes be enough?" He did not take his glittering eyes from her.

It was all Tabitha could do to prevent her smile from broadening, but she was determined and shook her head. She would not fall victim to his charms, no matter what.

"Sixty minutes?"

Tabitha laughed, and the three ladies nearest them stared at her. "No, Axwick."

The dance began. The ladies stepped forward with their arms outstretched and turned around their partners. As Tabitha's gaze circled the room, she could see with dismay Miss Theodosia Ashbrooke and Mrs. Bryant were both pointing and staring at her—two of the biggest gossips in Bath.

"I appear to be causing quite a scene by standing up with you," she murmured dryly, at a point in the dance close enough to converse without being overheard. "Should I be concerned of any dark secrets in your past?"

She returned to her place in the set, and the gentlemen moved as one toward the ladies.

"No," said Axwick shortly. "As part of my vow never to wed, I have not danced for the last three years."

Her face tightened with shock as they clasped hands with the pair beside them.

"I am..." She tried again in a low whisper, "I am the first woman you have danced with...in three years?"

He nodded as they changed direction, and Tabitha tried desperately to concentrate on the dance as emotions churned within her, overwhelming her and forcing her into silence.

The first woman he has danced with for over three years? No wonder the gossips of the *ton* could not stop staring at her! Why was he singling her out? He must have a reason. She barely knew him, but she could tell Richard St. Maur never did anything without due consideration.

They parted and circled back to their places. Despite the slowness of the dance, Tabitha's heart was pounding. Could this mean...was it possible Axwick was changing his mind about marriage?

He stepped toward her with hands outstretched, and she took them, as was expected in the dance. What was not expected was the sudden shudder of heat between them. She looked quickly into his eyes. He had felt it, too.

"Do you want to get married one day?" The question from Axwick was abrupt, and he dropped his gaze.

There was not enough air in the room to breathe, but Tabitha managed to answer in a hoarse voice, "Yes. Yes, I do."

It was impossible not to blush. They were parading slowly through the set, arms entwined, hands clasped, and it felt almost like a proposal. Her reason told her it was a mere question of curiosity, and that was all.

Surely, that was all?

As they reached the end of the set, they took their respective places, and while everyone watched the next pair, Tabitha and Axwick simply stared at each other.

A question was burning in Tabitha's heart. "Have you ever considered it? Since taking your vow, I mean."

She made a conscious effort not to hold her breath as she waited for his answer. Axwick did not move, and in the intervening seconds, she wondered if he had even heard her. His eyes moved purposely down her body.

"No," he said finally in a low voice, eyes returning to hers. "I will never marry."

"Why?"

She wanted to rush toward him and take him by the hand, lead him somewhere they could talk in private. There was such depth to him. A depth she had never seen in another gentleman before. Something had happened to Axwick. Something dark and destructive, and it had destroyed a part of him, even if he did not know it.

At the exact moment he opened his mouth, the dance ended, and the room erupted with applause.

Axwick closed his mouth with a smile and bowed. Tabitha replied with a curtsey, but by the time she had risen, he was standing before her and had taken her hand in his.

He did not speak. They walked away from the crowd, feverish mutterings and pointing following them as they passed. Tabitha had no idea where he was taking her, but something about the set of his jaw told her this was not the time to ask questions.

They passed through the door into the hallway, mercifully quiet as the ball was at its height. A clock was chiming a quarter to midnight.

Lady Romeril's architect had spared no expense, and in the latest fashion, she had ordered pillars to be added to her hallway. Axwick led her to the one furthest away from the ballroom and pulled her behind it so they were hidden from those passing through the hallway.

"I have no wish to lie to you," he said in a low voice, staring at her as though attempting to read her mind.

"I have no wish to be lied to," she breathed.

In the silence of the hallway, she could hear his ragged breathing. For the first time in their acquaintance, he was not controlled.

"There are things about my family…" Axwick coughed and shook his head. "My mother was a good woman. She deserved better than my father. He drank, Miss Chesworth, and far more than was good for him."

Tabitha saw the pain in his eyes and knew if she were to speak, he would stop.

"She had but three consolations in life, and they were her children," Axwick said with a wry smile. "Arnold, Charlotte, and myself. My brother ascended to the dukedom three years ago and repaid my mother's love, care, and concern with the decision to not only follow in my father's footsteps, but to add gambling to his list of sins. We almost lost everything, and my mother…she died two years ago from a broken heart."

Tabitha's heart broke in turn. There was such tenderness in his voice, such heart-wrenching sadness as he spoke about his mother—and such controlled fury as he spoke of his brother.

"The more I examined my family history, the more I saw it," Axwick continued bitterly. "Every man in the Axwick line was weak, and either drink or gambling was his downfall. No more. There will be no more Axwickes after me."

Tabitha attempted to collect her thoughts and consider what the best thing to say was. She opted for the truth. "You surprise me," she said softly. "I have never heard anything about this."

Axwick laughed. "Yes, I have spent much time and a little coin in hiding the truth from society, but some news always gets out. The last three years have been consumed with tracking down all of my brother's debts and paying them off."

"That was most noble of you. You were under no obligation to do that."

She watched the twin emotions of pride and shame battle across his face.

"It was a debt of honor," he said finally, "and I could not allow it to continue—just as I will not allow the male line of the Axwickes to continue. It ends with me."

Tabitha smiled sadly. "And that, I think, is a great shame."

"You think so?" Axwick stared at her with an appraising look and took her hand in his. She tried not to gasp aloud at the spark of heat pouring into her body as he continued. "But that does not mean I cannot have any…fun, Miss Chesworth."

She wrenched away her hand, scandalized at his insinuation—and even more troubled to find herself intrigued by his words. If only there was a way for a gentlewoman like herself to find out more of what he meant without opening herself to accusations of wantonness.

"Come now, Tabitha," Axwick spoke low as he stepped forward, "let us be people of the world."

She stepped back, eyes locked on his, unable to look away, and felt the cool marble of the wall behind her. She was pinned against it and was even more trapped when Axwick raised his left hand to the wall beside her.

"I knew from the first instant I saw you that I wanted to make love to you," he murmured, moving so close, she could not move an inch without pressing up against him.

She gasped at his words and attempted to brush past him.

"Axwick, let me—"

"Richard," he whispered, and the single word caused heat to wash over her. "Call me Richard, and I might let you go."

Tabitha licked her lips nervously, and he groaned, leaning toward her and pinning her against the wall. She could feel the strength of his body, the heat of it, and desire poured from his eyes.

"Richard," she said clearly. "Please let me…"

But her words were stopped by a finger he placed on her mouth. "You will bring someone over here if you are too loud, and how would we explain this?"

His voice was caressing. Her pounding heart battered against her chest. Heat and desire were washing through her body. It was thrilling, being penned in like this by his strong arms, and it stirred something disgraceful in her imagination.

"Better." Axwick removed his finger and placed his hand on the wall again, trapping her more completely.

She wanted to be free but also wanted to be close to him.

"I am not interested," she said in a shaking voice, "in one night of passion."

Axwick smiled deliciously. He shifted his stance so that he was leaning against her.

"That is not what I offer," he whispered. "One night of passion? Tabitha, you are worth far more than that. No, I want to bed you night after night, bringing you to endless pleasure. Pleasure you have never known before. Pleasure you may never know again."

She licked her lips once more, but this time, unconsciously at the thought of Axwick's hands on her.

"This is a serious offer, one I am sure you will not refuse."

Her head arched away from him. The feeling of his breath on her neck was overwhelming, and she tried desperately to think, but all she could do was feel him pressed up against her, feel the hardness between his legs against her stomach. It was impossible to breathe at the thought of him pleasuring her.

He moaned and dropped his head. "Oh, God, Tabitha, I could give you such pleasure. Why not let me show you?"

Before she could say anything, before she could even think, he pressed his lips against the side of her neck, just below her ear. Something broke between them, and his hands dropped from the wall and grasped either side of her waist.

"Tabitha, I want you," he moaned into her ear. "Let me make love to you. I can make you cry out again and again until…"

She broke away, twisting and almost stumbling. Her body was on fire for him, but she could not let him say such things.

She put a hand to the pillar to steady herself and saw the untamed desire in his eyes.

Axwick leaned against the wall as though exhausted, a curl of hair falling across his face. "That is my offer, Tabitha, and I beg you to take it."

She swallowed and managed to say before she strode away to the safety of the dancing, "If you want to make love to me, you will have to marry me first."

CHAPTER SIX

RICHARD COUGHED. A carriage rattled behind him, and a gust of February wind blew through him.

This was ridiculous. What on earth was so difficult about taking a few steps?

But it was more than that, he reasoned with himself. Seven steps, to be exact. He had calculated the number in the ten minutes he had been standing here like a complete fool. Yet, those steps into the Pump Room were the longest distance in the world.

He could not remember being nervous like this before. Even being the lead pallbearer at his brother's funeral had been easier.

A pair of ladies stared, curiosity etched across their faces. One of them looked back after they passed him.

Richard nodded curtly. Before, he would have taken a good look at a pair of young ladies.

Now, all that consumed his mind was two nights ago at Lady Romeril's ball with Tabitha. He did not even need to close his eyes to be taken back. She had quivered against him, and he had felt her repressed desire, her fear, her anticipation of what he would do next.

She had been in his power, and the certainty of her determination not to be seduced by him… It was intoxicating, every second he shared with Miss Tabitha Chesworth. He had wanted to follow her, but something had held him back. It had taken all of his self-control to prevent himself turning up outside her home the next day. It would not have taken Matthews long to discover her address, but what then? No, restraint was the only choice, for who knew what he may have said, may have promised, in that heady intoxication of her body.

Today was today, and he was sure she—like all good society wintering here in Bath—would be attending the Pump Room.

He had always been sure of what he wanted and taken it. Or it had been offered to him.

If only Tabitha would accept his offer.

"Excuse me, sir, but is the Pump Room closed?"

A gentleman he did not recognize was staring with a concerned furrow of the eyebrows.

"Closed?"

"Closed," repeated the gentleman with a confused smile. "Have they not opened the doors?"

Before he could reply, the doors opened and three ladies left, inclining their heads to Richard and the stranger.

Richard smiled weakly as they passed, but instead of returning his smile, the man stared at Richard as though he were weak minded and stepped around him and into the warmth of the building.

"God's teeth," cursed Richard under his breath, shaking his shoulders to try and keep them warm. He was not a coward; none of his acquaintances would ever describe him as such. If he wanted to bring Miss Tabitha Chesworth to his bed, then he needed to move.

"Richard St. Maur, the sixteenth Duke of Axwick," boomed the Master of Ceremonies as he finally entered the rooms nearly thirty minutes after he had arrived.

Each person who entered was announced. But since his name had not been spoken there in years, heads turned, and a group of gentlemen from Oxford beckoned to him, but Richard barely noticed them. He was scanning the crowded space to spy just one person. When he found her, she did not react to his presence at all.

Tabitha was wearing an elegantly fitted, cream muslin gown with a matching bonnet, earnestly in conversation with a young man he did not know. Rage flooded into his mind, heart, and stomach, which wrenched at the sight of her with another man.

Why did she not want to speak with him? Why didn't his name, called out across the room, cause her to turn around? It was a blow to his pride.

The gentleman said something, and Tabitha laughed. Richard clenched his hands with irritation. Who was this stupid man? A brother, a cousin?

If only it could be so. That was a very unbrotherly look he was giving her.

Unable to think and filled with a possessive need to be with her, Richard tried to collect his wits, but damn the man to hell, even if he did have the right to speak with her. She was not the duke's to protect, but he wanted her to be. By God, he wanted her to be.

"Axwick, I thought it was you!" Josiah Stanhope, Earl of Chester, strode toward him with a smile. "I did not know you were in Bath, though I did hear some chatter about you standing up at a ball! Tell me, is it true?"

At any other time, Richard would have grasped the hand of his old friend, or at least given a deep bow to Chester.

But not today. Tabitha was being utterly charmed by another man, and he would not stand it. He strode past Chester without acknowledging him, his need to be with her completely overwhelming.

It took less than a minute to wend his way through the crowd, and as he reached her, he said without thinking, "Tabitha."

"—and I said—oh. Good morning," she said.

The gentleman stared at Richard, evidently astonished anyone could be so rude as to march up to a conversing couple, ignore the gentleman, and blurt out the young lady's name without a hint of decorum.

Richard did not care. All his attention was on Tabitha, and she colored at the intensity of his gaze and curtseyed.

"Your grace," she said demurely, eyes downcast.

"Your—your grace?" The gentleman looked from one to the other and stiffened as he took in his expensive, silk cravat, elegantly styled hair, and gold signet ring. "To whom do I have the honor of addressing?"

Richard's eyes snapped to the gentleman in surprise, as though suddenly realizing he was there, but he said nothing.

Evidently, this was expected of nobility by the gentleman, as he did not seem offended but rather impatient to make his acquaintance.

"Mr. Charles Lister, your grace," he said, bowing deeply.

Richard took in the *nouveau riche* waistcoat, the collar points clearly attached to the shirt through buttons rather than a true linen collar, and the hints of ink around his fingertips. Trade, then, most likely an educated one.

He turned back to Tabitha. "Miss Chesworth, I must speak with you. Now."

Her green eyes sparkled as she said with an obvious attempt at blandness, "Ah, but I am currently speaking with Mr. Lister."

Her hands were clasped before her, holding onto her reticule, and she gave a hint of a smile, telling him she knew exactly what she was doing.

Richard grinned, a smile which had felled and bedded several women in the past. "I would appreciate it, Miss Chesworth, if we could speak alone. Just for one minute."

"And I would appreciate it if I could continue to speak to Mr. Lister about the *fascinating* trip he took with his aunt just last month to Newcastle, your grace."

God in heaven, but there was no one like her. Her eyes shone with amusement as he struggled with his emotions. Richard could not manage the conflict warring inside his heart, yet was impressed at how content she was toying with him in public.

He had forgotten this feeling, this flurry of emotions, the thrill of the chase. As a duke's son, then a duke's brother, and now a duke himself, he could not recall the last time he had struggled to convince a beautiful woman to give herself to him.

Until now.

"So, tell me, Mr. Lister," Tabitha said, turning back to the man. "What response did you receive when you made the offer on the racehorse when you were in Newcastle?"

"Ah," said Mr. Lister, a little unsure as he looked between them, but Tabitha was smiling with such sincere interest that he had no choice but to continue. "Well, I made sure my offer was intentionally low at the beginning of the conversation, naturally, to give myself more room to bargain later, and—"

"That was a risk," Richard interrupted, his eyes not moving from Tabitha. "Not every offer can be made twice."

Tabitha glared at him with an eyebrow raised and turned back to Mr. Lister. "And what happened next?"

Mr. Lister stared at Richard, trying to understand the interruption. "But your grace, I fully intended to make the offer again. You have to assume any offer made to you will only be made once, that is common sense, but I always intended to keep offering slightly higher if I had not been accepted. The horse really was a champion, sired by—"

"I think you and I are very different," cut in Richard. "When I make an offer, I expect it to be accepted. I am not in the habit of making second ones."

Mr. Lister gaped. "But…well, your grace, if I may say so, I would consider that short sighted."

"I could not agree more with you, Mr. Lister," said Tabitha smoothly, her eyes flickering to Richard. "Do you expect, your grace, that your offers will be so superior, they will never be turned down?"

Richard took a step forward, desperate to be closer to her and hating the dratted Mr. Lister's presence as Richard and Tabitha secretly spoke of his offer made to her just two nights ago.

"Naturally," he countered. "My offer has never been turned down before."

Tabitha laughed. "There is a first time for everything."

"And yet, denial has merely made me more determined to be accepted," he said, his voice dropping in volume.

Tabitha stepped toward him. "You must set much by your powers of persuasion."

"I have never found myself very persuasive," said Mr. Lister helpfully, attempting valiantly to rejoin the conversation, but it was impossible. Richard had only eyes for Tabitha, and she was utterly bewitched by him.

"I am more than ready," Richard was speaking in such a low voice full of meaning that no one save Tabitha, could hear him, "to rise to the challenge to ensure my offer is accepted."

"I think you should be prepared to be disappointed," she said.

"Actually, I was not disappointed," said Mr. Lister, assuming her comment was addressed to him. "Because the horse dealer—"

"Because there are very few offers which cannot be ignored," continued Tabitha with a wry smile. "And I doubt whether you, Axwick, could make one."

Richard could feel the ache for her growing, and he could no longer continue with this battle of wits and words before the ignored Mr. Lister.

"Tabitha, please, may I speak with you?" he hoped the desperation he felt was not discernable in his words. He just fell short of pleading.

"No," she said simply. "There. Another way for you to accustom yourself to being disappointed. Your grace, you may not know me very well, and so I shall forgive you your ignorance, but you will soon learn I am not to be easily defeated."

No, you are not, Richard thought in wonder. What had merely been a pretty face was now turning out to be something far more interesting. A woman with intellect, wit, and no compunction in holding her own.

"I have come here on purpose," Richard found himself confessing, "to speak with you. Just five minutes."

She gazed at him appraisingly, and he saw a flicker of curiosity spark in her eyes, but before she could respond, another voice spoke.

"Actually, your grace," said Mr. Lister more sharply than before, "I would like to speak with you. For five minutes? Outside?"

Richard stared in astonishment. In all his exchanges with Tabitha, he had forgotten Mr. Lister. Intrigued by what this man could possibly want with him, and frustrated by Tabitha, he nodded.

"Five minutes," he said curtly and turned to Tabitha. "And then I will be back for you."

CHAPTER SEVEN

TABITHA STARED CURIOUSLY as the two gentlemen wove their way through the crowded room, disappearing from sight through the impressive doors.

Sparring with Richard for five minutes had given her more joy than speaking with Mr. Lister for the last twenty.

Raising a hand to her chest, she ignored the inquisitive looks wondering why the two gentlemen who had been conversing with her had abruptly departed together.

A duel, perhaps? Tabitha almost laughed aloud. Gentlemen did not fight duels, not anymore, and certainly not over ladies they had only just met! So why the conversation outside, and without her? She had not thought they were acquainted, and yet something had obviously occurred that required Mr. Lister to speak with the duke privately.

She was starting to draw attention to herself by standing alone. After a genteel cough, Tabitha promenaded around the room, joining the flow of the crowd, but the conversation she was not part of never left her mind.

Tabitha walked nonchalantly out of the Pump Room.

"Here she is," a young woman giggled as she jumped into Tabitha's path, arm in arm with another young lady, neither of whom Tabitha knew. "Here, Mary, this is the bridesmaid I was telling you of! Miss Chesworth, is it not? Mary, this lady—"

"You must excuse me," Tabitha interrupted, heat rising in her cheeks as if they were watching an exhibit in a traveling circus. "I must speak with my friend."

Ignoring the cries of "Wait!" and "Miss Chesworth!", Tabitha inclined her head to the master of ceremonies as she stepped onto the abbey churchyard.

As she shivered in the cold winter air, Tabitha could not see either gentlemen, but in the quiet of the morning, she heard voices around the corner on Stall Street.

Shocked at her daring and trying to convince herself this was not eavesdropping, as anyone could walk by and accidentally overhear their conversation, Tabitha crept behind one of the pillars so conveniently hiding her from Mr. Lister and Axwick.

"—back off I say," Mr. Lister said in a low and urgent tone. "I will not ask you again, sir, I am telling you. Back away from young Miss Chesworth."

Tabitha gasped and bit her lip. She did not want to give herself away, not now that she knew exactly what their topic of conversation was.

"I have no idea what you are talking about," Axwick's voice said curtly.

Mr. Lister laughed. "Oh, but I think you do, sir, and I would remind you that I got here first. I saw her in the Pump Room, and I was the one which spoke to her. Miss Chesworth is mine to have, 'tis my right."

Tabitha's eyes widened. To hear herself spoken about…What was Axwick's reply?

"I beg your pardon," came the cold words, "but I do not believe—"

"Do not think you can fool me, Axwick, for I have heard of you," Mr. Lister interrupted. "I know exactly what your plan is, and I can tell you, it will come to naught. 'Tis Miss Chesworth's dowry, is it not? Come now, sir, as soon as I heard your name, I understood it all. You think there is a soul in Bath who has not heard of your money troubles?"

There was silence and, despite Tabitha's growing curiosity, she dared not chance peeking around the pillar to see the look on Axwick's face.

"There is no shame in it," Mr. Lister's voice sounded easy and relaxed, while Axwick was conspicuous only in his silence. "We are not so different, you and I. Why do you think I am interested in Miss Chesworth in the first place?"

Tabitha flushed with embarrassment. She had never considered Mr. Lister as a suitor, so his treacherous nature was no loss, but it was mortifying to discover he was only interested in her for her inheritance.

"Yes, her father left her quite the fortune," Mr. Lister had continued. "Thirty thousand pounds! Despite the fact she's a little chit with more trips down the aisle than most vicars," and he laughed into the quiet, "I am more than willing to take her down once more, for that amount of cash."

A crash echoed across the street, and Tabitha heard a grunt which she could not understand. Swallowing hard, she risked a peek around the pillar.

And what a sight to behold. Mr. Lister, grunting and turning red, was pushed against the wall by his collar by none other than the Duke of Axwick.

"What the—" Mr. Lister spluttered, his voice hoarse, and his face starting to darken as Axwick increased the pressure around his neck. "What the devil d-do you think you—"

"Stay away from her." Axwick's words were hissed with such anger and vehemence that Tabitha shivered. "Stay away from Miss Tabitha Chesworth."

Mr. Lister's hands were scrabbling against Axwick's, but it was no use. The duke was far stronger, and he had no trouble in keeping the irate man against the wall, even as his feet started to kick.

The duke lowered his face toward Mr. Lister, and there was real hatred on his features. "Tabitha deserves someone who cares for her," he said quietly with menace. "Not some idiot who wants her money to waste on horses."

Mr. Lister's face almost turned purple as he managed to say, "Why do you care? Is she under your protection?"

Tabitha's gaze shot from Mr. Lister to Axwick, who dropped his hold on the gentleman. Mr. Lister sank to his knees, clutching at his throat.

The duke took a step back and stared at Mr. Lister. "Yes."

Tabitha tried to slow her breathing. It was thrilling to watch such a man defend her, to claim her for his own in such a way, and to see a man like Mr. Lister get what he deserved for speaking of her like that.

But it was not over. As Axwick turned away from him, Mr. Lister rose shakily to his feet and spat on the ground.

"I should have known," he said darkly. "I should have known the whore was spoiled goods."

Tabitha's scream was unheard, covered by the echoing sound of a fist crunching into a cheek.

Axwick punched him cleanly, and his head spun back and hit the wall. Blood spurted from Mr. Lister's nose, and his hands flew to his face as he let out a cry of agony.

Breathing heavily and staring stoically at the groaning man collapsed on the ground, Axwick spoke in a dark but controlled voice, "Miss Tabitha Chesworth," taking in another breath, "is as pure as the Virgin Mary. But I care for her, you understand, and I will not permit anyone disgusting or repellent, such as yourself Lister, to speak ill of her or pursue her. She deserves better, and by God, I will make sure of it."

Mr. Lister was gazing at the duke with a mingled look of fear and horror. There was a bruise starting to darken on his cheek that was remarkably like Axwick's signet ring but in reverse.

"Y-you are mad," he said, shaking his bleeding head and struggling to his feet. "Mad, I tell you, to protect a woman who is neither family, nor fiancée, nor mistress! Why…"

Axwick took a menacing step forward, and Lister broke off, stumbling to the side and staggering away. Axwick leaned against the wall, still breathing heavily, his eyes downcast as though he was carrying the weight of the world on his shoulders.

Tabitha's heart was in her mouth, and she was breathing just as heavily. Why would he do such a thing? To fight a man, to attack him in such a way, leaving him under no illusion that she was under his protection, that her honor was his own.

Why would he do that if he had no honorable intentions toward her?

Something like hope, or a feeling very close to it, rose in her chest. It was shocking to see such violence and on the streets of Bath, too, a civilized city!

There was something animalistic in his act, something territorial, instinctual. It made her shiver all over. If only she could know exactly what he was thinking, for she had the same question as Mr. Lister. Why would a gentleman, and a duke no less, do such a thing? Stake his own reputation like that for a lady with whom he was entirely unconnected?

Tabitha stared at him leaning against the wall, and before she could hide herself behind the pillar once more, Axwick saw her.

His eyes widened, and he stood up straight immediately. Embarrassment warmed Tabitha's cheeks, their eyes unable or unwilling to separate.

"R-Richard," she stammered.

Perhaps it was because his temper was already up that made him do what he did next. Perhaps it was the shock of seeing her there, after speaking of her so passionately and determinedly. Perhaps it was because she had used his name, the name which she had refused to use since they had met.

Perhaps it was a fiery medley of all three. Whatever the reason, Richard strode forward with that fierce look, covering the yards between them so quickly that Tabitha could not move or make a sound, and before she knew what was happening, he had grabbed her arms, pushed her roughly against the pillar she had hidden behind, and kissed her passionately on the lips.

Oh, and what a kiss. As his lips touched hers, she was overcome with longing, longing that he awoke in her but she had not understood. His lips had captured hers instantly, and the shock of pleasure that rippled through her body was made all the sweeter by the softness twinned with the barely controlled desire she could taste.

His hands tilted her head, and Tabitha's eyes closed, utterly lost in the kiss. It deepened as his tongue gently pried her lips open, and she welcomed him in, welcomed the fire burning through his body. She did not have to think, just feel, and it felt right to raise her hands to his head to pull him closer, it felt right that he was pushing her against the pillar, entrapping her between the cold marble and the blazing heat of his body.

Her tongue, gentle and curious, met his own, and Richard groaned in her mouth. This was fire, fire like Tabitha had never known, and she could not tell whether she was the flame that set him alight, or if he was the blaze burning her. They kissed until they ran out of air and were forced to break apart.

Tabitha opened her eyes. His face was close to hers, his hands on her hips.

She wanted to say something about the way she felt, about how he was making her melt inside, but before she could, he spoke.

"I-I am sorry," he said in a jagged voice.

Tabitha blinked, drunk on desire. "Why?"

Richard laughed bitterly and drew his head away from hers. "I…I am far more in your power than I thought, Tabitha. I should not have been so despicable in the Pump Room."

His dark eyes looked hungrily at her, while his words were so remorseful. She could not help but laugh. Her hands left his face and found his hands on her hips, entangling his fingers between hers.

"I am glad," she said simply. "I know what Mr. Lister is truly like, and I have you to thank."

"You are far too good for a man like Lister," Richard growled.

Her heart had been racing since she had seen Richard punch Mr. Lister for her honor, but it quickened again at her daring.

She smiled and tilted her head. "Am I too good for a man like you?"

Something fired in his eyes, and he leaned forward to kiss her, but Tabitha placed a finger on his lips this time.

"That," she whispered, wishing she was not about to say these words, "was not an acceptance of your offer. I spoke the truth before. If...if you want to make love to me, you will have to marry me."

Tabitha thought she had finally gone too far. He would surely step away from her, angry she had led him to believe he could have her.

Richard took her wrist and pinned it to the pillar. Before she could react, he held both hands above her head.

She gasped, her whole body covered by the strong hardness of the Duke of Axwick.

He moved his head closer to hers, and Tabitha arched instinctively to kiss him, but he drew back just enough so she could not reach him. Now it was her turn to feel hungry for the sensation of his lips on hers, but she did not have the words to explain it—begging him for the one thing she wanted so badly. There was something happening between her legs—a hot sensation.

"Someone could walk by," she whispered as she strained against his hold. "They would see us, and you will have missed your chance, Richard. You will miss your chance to taste me again—"

If it had been anyone else's words, they would have mortified her.

With Richard, it felt natural.

His response was even better.

"I will kiss you when I am damn ready." He leaned closer.

Tabitha went to meet him, mouth open for the kiss, but he leaned back again, and she moaned with frustration.

"God, Tabitha," he muttered, his eyes flashing. "Though I would be glad to find my way into your bed, the idea of finding my way into your heart is not as repellent as I had once thought."

She fell in love with him then, her whole being tumbling over a cliff. She could only hope he would be there to catch her.

"Richard," she cried into his mouth, and he pushed her harder against the pillar, his lips finally crushed against hers.

And then it was over. The sound of footsteps echoed down the street, and he released her hands and stepped away. She could still feel the pressure of his lips on hers, still taste him.

A young woman wearing spectacles walked past them, a disapproving expression on her face. As she reached the end of the street, she peered back and shook her head before turning the corner.

Tabitha tried to calm her breathing.

"I could do that all night," he said, staying a few steps away from her. "And more, Tabitha. Damn it all."

The temptation to say yes and take me with you, to show her all the delightful things a man and a woman could do to each other, almost overwhelmed her. But she hesitated. She had to be strong, she could not allow herself to be easily won. If she was truly a prize worth fighting for, she had to be worth waiting for.

"I know you could," she said lightly. "I know."

Without saying another word, she walked away, unsure of anything except that this was the right thing to do.

He was the one in her power.

CHAPTER EIGHT

R ICHARD HAD NEVER thought the library clock had a loud chime. He kept it because it had been his mother's.

Despite its subtle noise, Richard jumped violently as it struck three. The book in his lap slipped to the floor, and he blinked, unable to remember what he had been reading. Picking it up, he saw it was *The Rime of the Ancient Mariner*. He opened it to the marked page and read the same verse again without taking in a single word.

He placed the book on the table and laughed.

He had never felt this way about a woman before, and it was frightening, exhilarating, and confusing. None had ever caused him such distress; no one had ever resisted him.

Every time he closed his eyes, it was not any of the women from his past. It was Tabitha he saw. He was kissing her passionately, and she smiled seductively and quivered as he touched her warm and glowing skin.

It was impossible to rid himself of her, and he did not want to.

Unlike every other encounter, a kiss was not enough, her touch was not enough, the wildness he could sense underneath her controlled facade was not enough.

He wanted to learn everything about her, know every part of her life that brought her to this moment. Richard chuckled as he shook his head. He barely knew anything about her.

Yes, she was passionate. She was determined, too, for few women could have rejected him after being intimate with him—it made him hard just thinking about it.

What was her history? Did she have brothers or sisters? What were her interests, what made her the woman he knew?

He could barely think straight after just two kisses. If they shared more, what would it be like for him—what dangers would he face?

Charlotte entered the room and laughed.

"This is the quietest I think I have ever seen you," she said lightly.

"'Tis not really what you expect from me, is it?"

She considered him carefully. "No. What is going on, Richard?"

He sighed, unprepared for the conversation. Charlotte may laugh, but she would never judge him.

"I think," he said carefully, startled at how difficult the words were, "I am having rather warm feelings for Miss Tabitha Chesworth."

Charlotte scrunched her nose. "Oh, Richard! I do not want to hear the sordid details of *that* part of your life!"

"No, no, you misunderstand me," he said quickly. "I mean…well, as surprising as this will be to you, Lotty, I…I think 'tis more personal than that. I mean to say…well. I actually like her."

Charlotte stared at her brother, then she sank into a chair. "I have never heard you speak like that about a woman before."

He laughed dryly. "I think if I am not very careful, I will be truly caught, and then where will we be?"

He hoped, though would never admit it, that she would say he was more than a match for Tabitha.

But she did not. "The question is," she said, looking serious, "when will you go to her mother and ask permission to court her? Because you must do it properly, Richard, if you hope to marry her."

Richard scrunched his nose the same way his sister had. It was a family trait they had learned from their mother.

"Never," he said curtly. "I need to bed her to get her out of my system. I suppose you would say a night with Tabitha is the cure."

Charlotte leaned back in her chair. "So, this is just the same as all the others, after all."

Irritation rose. Could she not see Tabitha was different? But then what did that mean? Would bedding her give him the relief he wanted? Did he want to be released from her at all?

"This is different," he said eventually. "I am not sure how, but it is different."

Somewhere in the depths of his mind, and he did not care to examine the thought more closely, was the wish it would not be the same. That he would want her, and she would want more than just a night of pleasure and passion.

Perhaps Tabitha could be…if not a mistress, then a companion for him. Not a wife, not a woman to bear him heirs and continue the accursed family line. But a woman he could make love to and find comfort with.

It was a far cry from his heady, youthful days when any woman was enough for the night, but he was older now. Wiser. Hungry for more. Hungry for her.

"So what is your next move?"

Charlotte's voice cut through his thoughts and Richard smiled. "Why? Curious?"

His sister shrugged. "Gentlemen make all of the decisions in courting. As it is unlikely to happen to me in any event, it would be nice to gain a view from the other side."

There was sadness in her tone but nothing but steel in her eyes, and Richard knew better than to attempt to comfort her. Lotty had never wanted pity, even when a child. She may only be a few years older than himself, but she had always been more controlled.

"I have already decided on my next course of action. I am to host a ball and invite Miss Chesworth. I think it unlikely she will refuse an invitation. Few would decline one from the Duke of Axwick."

Charlotte started to laugh but stopped when he did not join in. "Y-

You are not serious?"

Richard nodded. "More serious than I have been about anything else."

"But you must see that hosting a ball is completely impossible!" Charlotte stared at him in amazement. "You have said yourself how delicate our financial situation is at the present time, and who knows how many more bills or debts from Arnold will arrive that we have no notion of! A ball? Our finances are in ruins and debts are undoubtedly owed to tradesmen across Bath and London!"

"Tabitha is worth the expense."

"I am not saying Tabitha is *not* worth it," Charlotte said gently, "even as I ignore the suggestion that a woman can be purchased in such a way. But Tabitha, for all I have heard of her and all you have said, is not one to be impressed by big shows of splendor."

Richard swallowed. He had not considered that.

"—and even more importantly," continued Charlotte, "she may not even be aware the ball is for her in the first place. I think you will find she just wants someone to care for her."

He thought about their encounter outside the Pump Room.

"That was not an acceptance of your offer. I spoke the truth before. If you want to make love to me, Richard, you will have to marry me."

The mere thought of her made him stir uncomfortably in his chair, but he was determined. A ball would be the perfect place for him to seduce her, finally, with the commitment of nothing more than a night of delectable and sordid pleasure.

After that...who knew? Perhaps he would be able to convince her to enter into an agreement that was more long term.

"I know what I am doing, Lotty," he said gruffly. "I can find the money from somewhere."

Charlotte shook her head with a smile. "There must be an easier way to spend time with a young lady. If a gentleman asked me to take a walk with him, or play cards, or talk about books, or—"

"Anything like that would be construed as courting," he interrupted with a wave of his hand. "I am not courting her, Charlotte. I do not intend to marry Miss Chesworth. She knows that."

His sister rolled her eyes and rose from the armchair. "If you keep saying that so determinedly, one day you may even convince your-self."

CHAPTER NINE

T HIS WAS NOT going well.

Richard tapped his foot impatiently and fought the impulse
to snap at the servant who once again offered him a glass of punch.
The last thing he wanted was a drink, and the longer he stood here like
an absolute fool, the more frustrated he became.

It had taken just over a week to organize the ball, a feat Charlotte
had not believed possible—but here they were. The Bath Assembly
Rooms had been unavailable, forcing him to half the guest list and host
it in their home, and despite the hours spent ensuring the best food,
hiring the best musicians, and shouting at his valet, Graham, to retie
his cravat…she had not come.

Richard glared at one of the servants hired especially for the ball,
who was returning with a bottle of wine, and the man swerved away.

What kind of a man was he, making others physically fear him
because one woman had not responded to his invitation? He had been
sure he would receive her acceptance that morning, and he had almost
knocked Matthews to the ground when the butler had brought in the
morning's letters.

But she had not replied, and he had been standing by the front
door for nearly an hour, hoping she'd appear.

"Axwick!" Montague Cavendish, Duke of Devonshire, strode into
the hallway and bobbed his head in a bow. "Now, I have never been
able to persuade you before, but I am sure at your own ball you

cannot refuse me! A hand of cards—perhaps two?"

"No, Cavendish," Richard said curtly. He had intended his gruff tone to dissuade the duke, but it appeared to have the opposite effect.

Cavendish smiled good naturedly, rising to the challenge. "Come now, Axwick, 'tis just a game! We will not even bring money into it, if you don't wish to…"

"I have never picked up a deck of cards," he said, his temper flaring. "And I will not now. Go and find better friends to play with."

Cavendish stared and shook his head as he left, offended by his host's words.

It was bad form to be short tempered with his friend, especially one whom he had known for years, as far back as Eton. A nagging panic gripped his gut. Tabitha was not going to come.

It was ridiculous, and Charlotte had told him so the minute he had suggested it. He'd been arrogant to believe he would be enough to tempt her! Even if she did not enjoy balls, surely his company, or the promise of his company, would be enough?

A pair of giggling ladies wandered through the hallway and snorted at the sight of him standing there alone.

Richard ignored them. Perhaps it had been the speed of it all. Under a week, that had been all the notice given to his guests. He was surprised so many of them had not already been engaged for other events, and a small part of him suspected that some of them had been but had cancelled for the honor of being invited by a duke, him no less.

Sometimes the family name, ancient and respected as it was, had its uses.

But it was not enough for Tabitha. He had wanted to give her the invitation in person and had attended the Pump Room the very next day, but she had not been there. He had even checked the subscription book and had not missed her.

In fact, he had gone there the next three days…to no avail.

Miss Tabitha Chesworth had not appeared, and Richard had put up with the indignity of standing in silence as gentlemen and young ladies stared at him.

Before he had met Tabitha, he would have appreciated the attention from the ladies. He would have found one willing to give him what he wanted, and that would have been the end of that.

Yet, his mind ran only on Tabitha. Was she avoiding him? Had she been offended by the passionate kisses he had stolen from her? Had she perhaps found a gentleman equally determined to make her happy and content to be taken up the aisle?

"Richard?"

It was rare he did not feel pleased to see his sister, but she was simply not the woman he wanted to see.

"Not now, Charlotte," he snapped.

Charlotte's eyebrows raised as she smoothed the creases in her gown. "You know," she said quietly so only he could hear her, "you are very lucky I love you, because there is Miss Chesworth."

Richard whipped around in the direction his sister was pointing.

She was beautiful. More than that, breathtaking. Tabitha stood in the doorway, her hair placed elegantly high on her head with a few diamond pins glittering in the candlelight. As she stepped into the hallway, Matthews carefully removed her pelisse to reveal a shell-pink gown that shimmered with silver threading and silk at the hem. A tiered, diamond necklace showed off her slim neck and her eyes...

Richard tried to breathe. Her green eyes were shining with such anticipation, it was all he could do not to rush over to her, take her in his arms, and ravage that delicious mouth.

She thanked Matthews, and he replied with words Richard could not catch. She laughed, and what a sound! It deepened his desire for her, not just for her body, but to be with her, to be the one making her happy, to be the one sharing her secrets.

"Umm..." Richard attempted to form a coherent thought.

His sister laughed and obviously had been waiting for him to speak. Tabitha looked up from Matthews and saw him and Charlotte standing together, and her cheeks flushed.

Was it too much to hope that he had elicited such a response? Richard's hands were clenched, and he forced himself to release them. This was no time for youthful panic. This was his ball, her ball, and his chance to win her.

Tabitha stepped forward and curtsied to Charlotte, who returned the gesture.

"I am glad you were able to come, Miss Chesworth," Charlotte said politely with a smile.

"I am aware I have not answered the invitation formally, Lady Charlotte, and I must apologize for it. I was called away to London the afternoon I last saw your brother."

She finally gazed at him, and a surge of pride overcame him at hearing her acknowledge him and for the evident embarrassment it had caused her.

"Your grace," said Tabitha, turning to her hostess once more. "I only returned this morning, and I was mortified to find your invitation had not been given the proper attention. It is very gracious of you to still receive me."

The two women spoke as relief washed over Richard.

She was not ignoring him or avoiding him. She had been neither offended nor repulsed by him. She had been in London.

"...pleasant to see you," Charlotte said. "You must come to dine with us sometime this week, Miss Chesworth, I—"

"Why did you go to London, Miss Chesworth?" The two stopped talking and stared at him.

"London?" Tabitha repeated.

He nodded. "To leave Bath in the middle of the Season. There may have been people here who missed your company. I believe there were."

Had he said too much? No, she had understood him. Her gaze dropped, but she did not step away from him or make any excuses.

"Richard," Charlotte murmured with eyes blazing. "You simply cannot accost your guests in the hallway and demand they tell you why..."

"I went to visit a friend," Tabitha answered. "A close friend, one whom I have wished to see for a long time."

"A gentleman friend?"

Her smile widened. "Perhaps. What difference would it make to you?"

Why does she have such an effect on me? Richard could not understand it. Dozens of chits had wandered in and out of his life, yet none had captured his attention like this. But none had looked up at him with eyes quite like hers.

"Your secrets are yours to keep, I am sure," he said, attempting to keep his tone light and playful. "But I would be grateful, Miss Chesworth—Tabitha—if you would keep me informed of any gentleman callers who start to pay their respects to you. I am...interested to know."

His words had quite an effect on the two women before him. Charlotte's jaw dropped, and she glanced around them to ensure no one else had heard his scandalous remark. Tabitha, on the other hand, had not taken her eyes from him. Her lips curled into a smile.

What made him say that? Richard was falling deeper into something he did not understand, and he needed to stop it. He needed to pull himself together.

"Would you like to dance, Tabitha?"

If Charlotte had looked shocked before, it was nothing to the incredulity now on her face. Tabitha flushed as he used her name in public.

"What is the matter, Miss Chesworth? You cannot refuse?"

He knew she would understand his reference and was not disappointed.

Tabitha had a wicked glint in her eyes. "Why, your grace, this is one of the few offers of yours I am more than happy to accept."

It felt like a bolt of lightning shot through his body as she took his hand. This made every pound spent on this ball worth the cost.

Every head turned as they entered the dance floor. It was strange. He usually commanded the attention, but he knew it was the rare beauty standing beside him.

The dancing had not yet begun, and Richard had instructed the musicians to not even consider picking up their instruments until he entered the room with a lady on his arm. Once it was clear he was ready, they played the opening notes to *The Maid of Bath*, and there was a rush to join the Duke of Axwick in the first set of the night.

He did not care about the other guests. Tabitha had captured his unwavering admiration and left him transfixed.

The dance began, and as they drew together in a line, Tabitha smiled at him.

"To tell the truth," she whispered, "I have not stopped thinking about our kiss."

Filled with fire at such words, Richard gazed at her with such intensity, he was surprised she did not burst into flames.

"And yet," he said in a low voice as they joined hands, "I have not stopped thinking about doing many other things to you."

Her innocent blush sent him over the edge. She had not dropped her gaze as she licked her lips slowly.

It felt like torture, a slow death not being able to speak to her privately, to touch her.

Without warning, he grabbed Tabitha's hand and pulled her away from the set. It caused several people to whisper things he did not care to hear.

"Axwick, where are we going?"

He did not answer as he pulled her through the crowd. Judging the reaction of his guests, they must think him as wild as his brother and father. But why should he give a damn? He was his own man.

He ushered Tabitha through the hallway and along a corridor, not stopping until they reached his library.

He locked the door and leaned against it.

She raised an eyebrow. "Should I be afraid of you, Axwick?"

"I thought you called me Richard now?" he asked, drinking in the sight of her.

"You are Axwick when you misbehave," she said with a smile. "Richard when you are being good."

Oh, to have her call his name in the throes of passion. He hardly knew whether he preferred Axwick or Richard.

Axwick when you misbehave, Richard when you are being good.

He groaned. "Tabitha, you have no idea what you do to me. As for locking the door, do you distrust me?"

She did not reply immediately, turning away to look around the room. "Why should I trust you at all?" She walked around the table in the center of the room. "I hardly know you. I know you are the sixteenth Duke of Axwick and have a sister. If you tell me more, I'll know if you are lying."

Richard swallowed. This was not the direction he wanted their conversation to go. The less she knew about his family, the better for them both.

"You have been more secretive," he countered with what he considered his most cunning smile. "For I do not even know whether you have siblings."

Her soft smile remained, and she finally broke their gaze by picking up a book from the table and flicking through the pages. The silence between them lingered, and Richard felt an overpowering need to fill it.

Eventually his patience was rewarded, and Tabitha lifted her eyes to him once more. "I am an only child."

Richard stepped forward, but Tabitha seemed to have expected that, and while still facing him, she moved around the table, keeping him at a safe distance.

"What about your parents?" he asked.

Tabitha hesitated at his question. "My mother's name is Mary."

"And your father?"

"Paul. He...he died ten years ago, when I was young."

Something cracked in her voice, and it jolted Richard's heart as he cursed himself for bringing up something painful.

"I am sorry," he said gently. "I did not mean to ask such a personal question. Forgive me."

He had started moving again, desperate to be near her, to comfort her, hold her, caress her, but Tabitha laughed and countered his every stride.

"You do not need to apologize," she said with an airy voice, placing the book on the table between them. "I mourned him little. He was a gambler and a reprobate."

Richard stopped dead in his tracks and stared at her, his feelings of lust transformed into compassion. What in God's name were the chances her father's sins were the same as his own family's?

"A gambler?"

Tabitha nodded. As she moved again, her gown rustled. "Yes. Despite many family members telling me I would end up the same..." She took a deep breath. "I have not. And I will never be like him. One's nature can be overcome."

Richard took an unconscious step back and lowered his head with a laugh. This similarity could never have been predicted. It was fate, perhaps something deeper.

All the fire left him, leaving him dangerously vulnerable. "It is good to hear such words."

Gentle hands enclosed his, and he was surprised to find that she had moved around the table.

"Why?" she asked.

Richard wanted to tell her everything. All he could do was stare, amazed by her sense of compassion.

"I can see the pain in your eyes. This has everything to do with you not wishing to marry—but you can overcome those fears."

For the first time in Richard's life, a woman felt right in his arms—

shared the same sorrows. Her warm fingers, heart, spirit, made him feel...

"Shall I tell you what I see?" she asked gently. "I see only strength in you, not weakness."

Richard laughed bitterly. "I am not strong where you are concerned."

"Then I will be strong for the two of us," Tabitha said with a faint smile. "I have never felt more empowered or alive than when I am with you—like I could accomplish anything."

Then she was kissing him, and Richard clutched wildly at her, desperate for her as though she was the only water in the world, and he was a fire that had to be put out. The passion he poured into the kiss nearly drained him. She clawed at his collar to bring him closer, as though it would never be near enough.

Richard groaned at the feel of her, his hands on her waist, tugging her toward him, luxuriating in the feel of her. His desire was so potent, she stepped back, into the bookshelves.

She gasped, and Richard chuckled, for she was once again trapped.

"Is this the same trick you play on all the women you seduce? Take them to the library?"

"Never," Richard breathed. "No, this is only for you."

He dipped his head to kiss her once more and felt the scrape of her nipples budding with desire in her gown. His hands slid from her waist to her buttocks, cupping them.

"Just for me?" she asked.

Richard moaned as he kissed her again and again, his lips moving to her neck and that delicate spot just below her ear he knew would make her arch into him. She did, and he glorified in her pleasure, in making her want him.

"God, Tabitha, just for you, always you."

She untied his cravat and it fell to the floor. His waistcoat gaped open, swiftly following the cravat, and he felt completely at her mercy.

She held his face steady between her hands as they drew breath, and she whispered, "No others from now on."

Richard could barely think. "No." He lowered his lips to hers.

Tabitha's hands clutched his back as his tongue teased more pleasure from her. His hands moved to the ribbon at the front of her gown. He pulled at it slowly at first, but as Tabitha moaned in his mouth, he tugged it roughly and pushed down the thin gauze sleeves, her elegant gown fell to her waist.

She could not contain her desire.

Richard knew he was lost—but he had been lost when she had taken his hands, or was it when they had kissed by that pillar the first time, or maybe when they had first danced? He did not know or care.

He exacted one final kiss before lowering his lips to her *décolletage*. His nimble fingers made quick work of the corset until it and the gown fell to the floor.

"Tabitha, you are so…"

But Richard could not finish the sentence, and instead, showed her with actions. He captured a breast with his hand and kissed her nipple.

Her nails scrabbled at his back. "Richard–oh yes!"

His tongue teased and flicked, his other hand caressed the other breast, his body thrust tightly against hers.

He lifted his head and stared into her face with a wicked smile. "Now, does Richard mean I am being good—or do I want you to call me, Axwick?"

"Pleasure me," she moaned, her hands pulling him closer. "Love me, Richard, love me Axwick…"

Her words were stopped by his possessive mouth, and she arched against him and raised one leg to draw him closer. With a great effort, Richard broke the kiss and stared into her eyes.

This was it. This was when he knew, beyond a shadow of a doubt, that she would say yes to his offer of seductive delight.

"Tabitha," he said in a ragged voice, trying to ignore the temptation to enter her right against the bookcase, "will you make me very happy?"

CHAPTER TEN

THERE WAS A loud pounding noise ringing in her ears, and Tabitha's mouth was open.

Will you make me very happy?

Richard was waiting for her answer. This was what she had always longed for but never believed would actually happen.

A proposal. A proposal of marriage from a man who genuinely cared about her, who evidently loved her. He wanted her, was so afraid of losing her that he had declared his love.

"Well?" Hix eyes fixated on her as his hands continued to caress her.

Tabitha smiled at the man who had once sworn to never marry. In his brown eyes she could see hope and lust and something else. Something very much like love.

She swallowed. "Yes."

Richard pulled her closer for a deep kiss, both passionate and reverential. They had made this pledge to each other and nothing could break that bond. They would grow old together. They would make a life together and—

But it was impossible to concentrate on her future happiness when her current pleasure was at such a pitch. Richard broke the kiss with a devilishly handsome smile.

"Come with me," he murmured, pulling her across the room.

As Tabitha picked up her dress and followed him, clutching her gown to her breasts, it did not even occur to her to insist they return to the ball. Why should she? Where else would she want to be in the world than in his arms, when she throbbed with desire for him?

Richard pulled a book from the shelf, and Tabitha gasped as a hidden door sprung open, revealing a narrow staircase.

"No one but servants use this," Richard spoke hurriedly as they climbed the stairs, "and they will all be at the ball."

A narrow corridor opened at the top of the stairs, dark, with doors leading off both sides of it. Richard threw open the first door and pulled her into a small room that appeared barely lived in.

And then he stopped. Tall as he was, Tabitha tilted her head back to look into his face, a shadowed medley of desire and hesitation.

Tabitha swallowed. There was little furniture in the room, but there was a bed. She knew what he wanted, and she wanted it, too, but were they so bold? It would not do to despoil a young lady; it was not respectable.

Her heart swelled with love. He was to be her husband. What was the purpose of holding back their love for each other, for want of a few weeks, a visit to a church, and a ring?

She allowed her gown to fall, exposing her breasts to him. A smile danced across her face as she reached out with a trembling hand to his chest.

Richard needed no further invitation. He let out a growl as he pulled her toward him, those strong fingers returning to her waist and his mouth pressing down upon hers. Tabitha gave herself willingly, for what could be more incredible than this, this feeling of oneness, of being close to the man you loved?

Richard took a step back from her, naked but for her undershift.

"Take it off."

His words were level, but the shudder of his body told her he was barely in control—and it made her smile. He may be more experienced than she was, but in this room, she was the one in charge.

"And what will you do to me," she whispered, "if I do not?"

How could she speak wantonly, with no thought to consequences? Something thrilled inside her to see the frustration spark in Richard's body.

He stepped toward her, but Tabitha was ready, taking a step back. "No. I get to decide."

Richard laughed as he shook his head. "God knows I wanted a woman who knew her mind, but I did not think it would be to torture me!"

The thrill of power and desire shot through her. She would do anything for this man, anything, but there was something even more delightful about forcing him to do something for her.

"Now," she said quietly, hardly knowing how she could be so brazen, "take off your shirt, Richard."

Desire pooled in his eyes. Without taking his gaze from her, Richard slowly unbuttoned his shirt and dropped it to the ground.

Tabitha nodded in approval. She had felt the strength of him when he had pushed her against that pillar, when he pressed himself against her in the library, but she could never have predicted such a chiseled body existed under that shirt. A smattering of dark hair crept across his broad chest and down toward a part of him she was longing to know better.

"I beg you," he said in a low voice, "please, Tabitha, I want to…why do you keep away from me?"

The desperation in his voice was genuine. She could step away and still retain her innocence…but why would she want to?

Her breath fluttering in her chest, hoping this was the right thing to do, Tabitha turned her back to the man she loved. She did not need to see Richard to sense the effect she was having on him. His groan echoed in the small room, and within a second of lightly dropping her undershift to the floor, leaving her completely nude, he had clasped her naked body to him.

Tabitha gasped at the feeling of his hands on her hips.

"You are more intensely beautiful than the sun," Richard whispered in her ear as his questing fingers fluttered to her waist, as though unsure whether he was now permitted to touch. "I could look at you all day, Tabitha, all day and never tire of you, because you are complete perfection."

Something was rising in her that she did not understand and could not describe, and she wanted more.

"Tabitha." Richard's voice lowered as his fingers started to caress, sparking intense arousal that made her weak-kneed. "I am going to kiss every single inch of you. But first, I am going to tease you."

Without any warning, his left hand moved to her breast, and his fingers grazed across her nipple as his other hand moved swiftly to cover that secret place between her legs.

"Oh!" Tabitha arched her back at the sudden pleasure.

"Just relax. Trust me."

Two fingers gently entered that wet place where suddenly her entire body seemed to exist. It was pleasure she had never experienced as his fingers moved slowly within her, and though he had promised her such things, Tabitha could never have imagined such wonder.

His other hand was not idle. It became stronger, teasing her nipple as his hand embraced her breast, his lips kissing her neck as waves of arousal moved from breast to that deepest part of her and back again.

"Richard," she moaned, and her voice spurred him on. Something was building inside her, and before she knew it, her body was exploding as her first climax overwhelmed her.

It was not until she opened her eyes that she realized they had been closed. Richard's strong hands were holding her up, and she had evidently lost all control as the ecstasy of the pleasure had taken her.

"That was…" she breathed, unable to think clearly, trying to calm her breathing. "That was…"

"Yes," murmured Richard in her ear. "Can you stand?"

Tabitha felt the strength in her legs returning. After she gave a brief nod, he released her, and she turned—and gasped.

He had removed his breeches and stood naked in the moonlight shining through the small window. She had never seen a man like this before. Of course, she had studied the great artists and thought herself prepared for such a sight, if she was to ever have the opportunity.

But Richard? There was something truly astounding about him, something so masculine. It was all she could do in her pleasure-sodden state to continue standing.

She did not even try to speak. Instead, she threw her arms around him and kissed him.

The warmth of his body made her moan in his mouth. The feeling of his erection pressed against her was everything that made a man, and she could not help but lower a hand to touch it.

"No!" Richard moved away from her, and embarrassment shot through her. It must have been obvious, for he immediately continued, "I…I want this to be wonderful for you, Tabitha."

"It already is," she breathed.

"But better than this. It…it may hurt a little."

She had been warned about it by women who had whispered things at parties, but she had not understood it then. He seemed…well, too large for…

"I trust you."

Before she could say another word, he had thrust her onto the bed and joined her, his chest pressed against her breasts, his hips against hers. Tabitha could barely think but did not need to. Everything was passion and ecstasy, and she needed nothing else.

That hot feeling was building in her again. "Oh, Richard!"

He shuddered against her and dropped his mouth to her breasts, tasting her, teasing her with his tongue, and she arched against him, clinging to him.

"Christ, you are so warm and soft," Richard said as he nestled himself between her thighs.

Tabitha had known the mechanics but could never have imagined such feelings. She did not have the words to ask for what she wanted, but she had to have it or she would die.

"I want more," she panted. "I want you!"

He raised his head, delight and desire sparking between them like lightning.

"Are you sure?"

Tabitha smiled in what she hoped was a seductive way. "Never more so."

Richard grinned. "Bloody hell, Tabitha, I had no chance with you, did I?"

He was hers and she was his, and they would make each other happy for the rest of their lives. "Never."

With a curse breathed into her ear as he gave in to his desire, Richard plunged himself into her. Tabitha gasped at the sudden intrusion and felt the twinges of pain she had expected—but she opened to accommodate him as he moved.

"Are you—are you—"

"Oh, yes!" She shifted her hips slightly to take him in deeper. "Richard, yes!"

He needed no other words. Dropping his lips to hers, he rocked his hips slightly, and she pressed into him, desperate for the feeling of him deeper, harder, and faster.

He understood. Leaving her mouth and cursing once more under his breath, she felt him shift his position, and all she could think of was the rhythm of his movement piercing her with pleasure and rocking her toward another wave of pleasure.

Her fingers clutched his back, her nails scraping his skin as she lost complete control. She shattered, and her cries pushed him over the edge. He exploded into her, and she collapsed onto the desire-soaked linens and held him as he fell into her arms.

CHAPTER ELEVEN

RICHARD RECLINED ON the pillows and blew out a slow breath. He heard the pounding of his heart like a storm battering a port. He had only one other sensation: the warmth of Tabitha nestled against his side. He smiled in the dimness of the room, consumed with happiness.

Had he ever felt this good before? Had he ever felt this close and connected to a woman?

There was something hot in his stomach, and it did not burn like desire, but warmed him like an open fire after a long winter day's hunt.

Tabitha shifted against him. No, it had never been like this before. This was new.

A twinge of fear soured his stomach. He had not used any protection—after swearing he would never find a wife, he had risked the chance of a child. But the odds were slim, surely. God would not be so cruel.

"Share your thoughts?"

Richard started and joined in her laughter. The last thing he wanted was to share the idea currently racing through his mind, untamed and unexplained.

It still shocked him that Tabitha had accepted his offer, happy to give up her hopes of marriage, her thoughts of wedlock and all it entailed, for the chance to let him love her. And love her he had, and fiercely. How many more opportunities would she have, as his mistress, to experience his lovemaking?

"I was thinking," he said softly, "that we must agree not to tell anyone about this. It must be a secret, you understand, a secret between us. You and me."

He glanced at the chestnut hair drifting across his arm and shoulder. Tabitha had a smile dancing on her lips. She was utterly at peace—as though she had found what she had been looking for, and knew she would never be parted from it.

"Of course," came the sleepy reply. "I am more than happy to keep it a secret, just between us."

It was not the response he had been expecting—or rather, it had been the one he had hoped for, but had not expected her to agree to so readily. To agree to be his mistress, to keep their dalliance secret and, his body shifting uncomfortably at the very thought, agreeing to the possibility of more in the future...

"Richard," Tabitha murmured sleepily, "what changed your mind?"

Richard shifted his arm, clasping that delicate waist and bringing her closer to him. He groaned slightly at the feeling of her breasts grazing his chest and tried to clear his head. This was important, this conversation. It would not do to grow hard again and find himself unable to even think, let alone speak.

"Knowing you has changed my mind about a great number of things," he said slowly. Although difficult to speak of such things, with her it was possible. "You were told you would become the same, had the same weaknesses as your father—but you have not. You said things of that nature can be overcome."

"I believe it," Tabitha said quietly. "Every word of it."

The one candle in the room guttered, leaving them in complete darkness.

"You will not hear me admit this very often, but I was wrong,"

Richard smiled into the gloom. "Although it sounds strange, hearing that a man's faults did not necessarily lead to the destruction of his child...to know the cycle can be broken, that it is not damnation to the next generation...well, 'tis given me hope. You have proved me wrong, and I have never been more grateful."

Tabitha chuckled and moved her arm to enclasp him. "And I have never taken more joy in proving you wrong."

Their bodies nestled together comfortably. "It made me wonder for the first time, whether... Whether marriage and a family may one day be a future I can hope for."

Richard held his breath after this statement. He did not want to mislead Tabitha, did not want her to misunderstand. It was a hope, and a hope for the future, and if he could consider himself marrying anyone, it was her. But this was not a proposal, and she had known that from the moment she had accepted his offer in the library.

But one day perhaps. A sudden vision of Tabitha by his side, dressed in all the finery a duchess deserved, sparked into his mind and caused a rush of joy—a rush further increased by the laughing child darting out from behind its mother's skirts. Tabitha's skirts. His child.

Richard glanced at the woman at his side who was deeply lost in thought.

"When I entered my twenties," he started in a low voice, "It sounds strange to say it, but I had high hopes of being a father. It was expected, even as the second son. We had but one spare, and my brother had not wed." The memory of the day that hope had all come crashing down jolted him painfully, and he had to cough before he was able to continue. "That all changed on the day I gained my majority. On that day I had expected a little more responsibility, a slight increase in my allowance—all the selfish things young men want."

He paused for so long he felt a nudge in his side.

"And?"

"And it was on that day I received neither power, nor wealth, but something much more important. Knowledge."

"Knowledge about your father?"

Richard sighed. "Yes and no. Knowledge about everything, about his gambling habits, his drinking, the way he treated my mother, and how it was not even unique. It was merely a repeat of his father, and his father before him. Something tainted the blood of our line, and all were wastrels."

Tiredness tugged at his eyes, but he would not close them. He would not allow the image of his mother that day to enter his mind. The trail of tears on her cheeks, the way her fingers tensed in her lap, the fear he, too, would take a fist to her for saying such things, such truths.

"That was not the worst," he said quietly. "I heard my elder brother had already taken such a path. It was in my father, in my brother, and so of course, it was in me."

Neither of them spoke until Tabitha said quietly, "It must have been a shock."

"I do not think there is anything more shocking for a young man to lose all respect for his father. To tell the truth, he has been a devastating influence on the family fortunes. 'Tis only due to our name and the history of that name that we still manage to garner any respect in the nobility."

"But you have been duke for three years. You must have gained back some respect, even if it is for yourself."

Richard laughed bitterly. "I think the respect I wanted the most was self-respect. The last few weeks has changed how I think about myself far more than the last three years."

He knew his words were inadequate, unable to describe what she had done for him, but he had to try. His hand gently caressed the small of her back.

"You have made me believe," he said quietly, "for the first time in ten years that perhaps being a father is not something I have to deprive myself of. Perhaps I do not have to shy away from it. Perhaps, one day, I can embrace it."

It felt strange to say such words aloud, a new kind of vulnerability. Tabitha chuckled against his side. Her hand moved and touched her stomach.

"Well, you never know," she said in a laughing whisper. "We may find out soon whether you shy away from it or embrace it."

Something lurched painfully in Richard's stomach: a mixture of fear, excitement, and confusion. But it died away. There was something so perfect about the two of them together. Something that allowed him to drift off to sleep without a care in the world.

CHAPTER TWELVE

S OFT LIGHT POURED lazily through a window with no curtains. The light reached a young woman lying under a blanket on a narrow bed.

Tabitha was dragged from sleep and into the cold of morning.

She opened her eyes. The light was far brighter than normal. Her dark, green satin curtains were not there. She was also not in her bed, and she had absolutely no recollection of how she had got here.

The sensation of rough linen sheets told her two things. Firstly, she was absolutely not at home. Secondly, she was not wearing any clothes.

This latter thought sparked her awake like nothing else could, and she sat up suddenly, looking around the strange room. There were no clues about the owner of the room, and bile rose in Tabitha's throat as she tried to keep her breathing calm. The memories of where she was and how she had got there would eventually surface.

She took a deep breath, clutching the blanket to her. What was the last thing she could remember?

Closing her eyes, she breathed out slowly. She had found the invitation to Richard's ball when she had returned home. That was it, she had rushed to get ready and found herself on the steps of his home within the hour. She had seen him, met his sister again, and they'd danced together.

Her hand burned at the mere memory of him holding it, the echoes of the musicians resounding.

The dancing had not continued long. He had dragged her to the library, kissed her like no one had ever kissed her, and asked her the question she had been desperately hoping he would.

Tabitha, will you make me very happy?

Her cheeks grew hot as the recollection of their lovemaking filtered through her mind, and her body arched at the memory of the wonderful things he had made her feel.

I am going to kiss every single inch of you. But first, I am going to tease you.

She drew her knees to her chin and pulled the blanket closer around her, attempting to block out the cold. A smile crept over her face. She was engaged. Engaged to be married, something she had thought would never come. Engaged to Richard, a man she truly loved! Engaged to the Duke of Axwick!

Her stomach lurched. Marrying Richard would not just mean becoming his wife. It would mean becoming the next Duchess of Axwick.

But where was Richard?

She glanced around. No clothes to suggest he had just left the room, no letter explaining he needed to go downstairs to greet someone, or even speak to his sister and explain their disappearance from the ball—a disappearance, now she came to think about it, which must have been commented on by his guests.

The Duke of Axwick left his own ball and in the company of a young lady?

There would undoubtedly be some talk, but there was nothing for it. She would have to endure it until the secret of their engagement could be told.

A sudden hope leapt in Tabitha's heart: could he have left his signet ring? It would make such a wonderful reminder of their engagement, even if she could not wear it in public. Just to have it would remind her of their mutual affection.

Holding the blanket to her, Tabitha left the bed and examined the room. It did not take long. There was no ring.

She returned to the bed. Why had he not waited for her to wake before he had left? Why had he not woken her himself?

What time was it? There was no clock, and the wintery daylight could mean any time. Perhaps Richard had not been able to wait. Perhaps he had urgent business to attend to.

He was the sixteenth Duke of Axwick, Tabitha reminded herself with a smile. He was a very important man.

She sighed. Rising to her feet and keeping the blanket wrapped around her for warmth, she moved to the window. It was only when she saw the stables, servants walking with purpose carrying heavy boxes or calling out instructions, that she realized she must be in a servant's bedroom.

At that exact moment, Tabitha heard the chimes. There must be a stable clock out of sight, and she counted the chimes—nine, ten, eleven.

Eleven o'clock! No wonder he had become bored of waiting for her to wake. She had slept the morning away—and how would she explain this to her mother, if she had gone upstairs at home to see how her daughter was recovering from the ball?

Tabitha dropped the blanket and started scrabbling into her clothes. To think she may be found out by her own mother just because she had slept too long!

It was awkward trying to tie herself into her corset. There was no looking glass in the room, and Tabitha felt uncomfortable at wearing her gown from the ball—but she had little choice.

All she had to do was creep downstairs, unseen save for a sympathetic servant who could ready the carriage, and take the back stairs at home so her mother would not see her. It was most rebellious of her. If she had heard of another young lady of the *ton* acting in such a way, Tabitha would have been scandalized.

Bloody hell, Tabitha, I had no chance with you, did I?

She smiled. He was worth it, her handsome and caring duke. The more she learned of him, the more she saw the damaged and broken man underneath the strong façade, the more she loved him. Every second with him was agony and ecstasy, and she craved him like nothing else.

The impossible task of getting home started here—she opened the door a crack.

Peeking out, she could see no servants. She walked along the corridor softly, grateful her dancing shoes of soft leather were silent, found the narrow staircase, and traipsed down, opening the secret door into the library.

The soft light poured into the large windows, and there was a fire in the grate throwing a brighter light around the room. All was quiet, and Tabitha breathed a sigh of relief as she closed the secret door and stepped into the room.

Lady Charlotte was seated by the fire, utterly absorbed by a book. Tabitha's mouth opened in horror—and Lady Charlotte looked up.

The book fell to the floor with a loud thud as Lady Charlotte exclaimed in a horrified voice, "Miss Chesworth!"

Tabitha flushed and dropped into an inelegant curtsey. "Lady Charlotte, I do apologize for startling you."

"B-but you—I thought you had gone home last night!" Lady Charlotte stared at her as though she was a ghost, and then pink crept into her cheeks as understanding dawned.

"You must not be mortified on my behalf, Lady Charlotte, although I...I thank you for your concern. Your brother Richard and I are...we have an understanding."

It was beyond frustrating she could not share the truth with Lady Charlotte, but Richard had been very clear: it was to be a secret. But surely his sister would understand what she meant?

But instead of rising from her chair and greeting her warmly like a friend, or even smiling and saying how happy the news of her brother's engagement made her, Lady Charlotte did neither. She did nothing at all. She simply sat there, staring at Tabitha.

"An understanding," Tabitha said quietly, in case the words had not yet sunk in. "He asked me a...a question, and I have said yes."

Lady Charlotte shifted in her chair uncomfortably. Tabitha found to her surprise that this irked her; was she not to be congratulated by her new sister?

"You are not pleased," she said quietly.

Lady Charlotte's smile did not waver, but her eyes looked concerned. "Do not misunderstand me, Miss Chesworth. I mean no disrespect by my silence. It is just...well, I know my brother, and please do not be offended when I say I likely know him better, and I believe I know exactly what sort of an understanding you have with him. I cannot help but say I am sorry for it."

Tabitha swallowed. It was impossible to deny that Richard had sworn never to marry, for had he not declared it to her the very first time they had met?

Just because his sister had not heard his new promises from his own mouth, that did not mean he did not say them—or mean them.

She smiled, though a little awkwardly. "Any gentleman is permitted to change his mind, Lady Charlotte."

"Indeed he is," agreed Charlotte too quickly.

A prickly sort of silence grew between them. Despite her words, it was clear Richard's sister was not convinced he would change his mind on this matter, and that she, Tabitha, was likely to be delusional.

She stifled a laugh. Delusional? How could she have misunderstood his words? Did his sister think she would have willingly given her body, her innocence, unless she had been offered marriage?

"I wonder," said Tabitha quietly, breaking the silence, "whether you could lend me a pelisse or greatcoat to cover my...my gown. And perhaps your carriage, so I can return home?"

The last thing she wanted were the gossips of Bath to see her returning home in a gown she had been wearing the evening before. She needed something to hide it, and she had not thought it would be too difficult a request, but Lady Charlotte had colored.

"I am afraid to say we do not have a carriage at present," she said awkwardly. "But I will ask Matthews to call one for you, and you may take your pick of any pelisse or greatcoat I can offer you."

It was a kind offer, but Tabitha did not understand why Lady Charlotte denied the existence of a carriage. She was the sister of a duke for goodness sake—and no carriage?

But there were more pressing matters to accomplish. She needed to return home.

"Thank you." She smiled graciously.

Lady Charlotte inclined her head in response and pulled at the bell by the fireplace. It was several minutes before any servant arrived, and they were uncomfortable ones. Tabitha had not been invited to be seated and so stood, while Lady Charlotte stared, completely dumbfounded.

Eventually Matthews opened the door from the hallway. "My lady?"

"Matthews," Lady Charlotte said with relief. "My friend Miss Chesworth stayed here last night as she was too fatigued to make the journey home. Please call for a carriage and arrange for her to borrow a pelisse or such like."

Tabitha flushed slightly at the lie she had forced Lady Charlotte to tell but smiled gratefully at the butler, who bowed.

"Miss Chesworth. If you will come this way."

Tabitha hesitated. She should explain herself better to Lady Charlotte. She should tell her the realizations Richard had come to, what they had shared about their lives, the honesty and vulnerability they had offered each other.

But Lady Charlotte was picking up her book from the floor where it had fallen and did not seem to have any interest in continuing their rather stilted conversation.

Tabitha curtsied and stepped to follow Matthews into the hallway. Before the door had closed behind her, she looked back and saw Lady Charlotte seated in the chair with the book in her lap, unopened. She was staring into the distance, and she did not look happy.

CHAPTER THIRTEEN

TABITHA SLIPPED AS she reached the bottom stair, the stone floor still wet from the morning's scrub. She hardly noticed. After an afternoon and evening of recovery, waking in her own bed had felt, somehow, wrong. Her heart had ached whenever she thought of what happened yesterday.

Every step and breath felt different. On entering the breakfast room, she attempted to calm herself, sure her mother would immediately suspect something—perhaps even the truth...

"I left the letter out for you," Mrs. Chesworth said absentmindedly.

Tabitha jumped as she dropped into a chair. "Letter?"

Her mother looked up from her breakfast with a confused expression. "I told you, I am sending a letter to Mabel—Mrs. Perry, as she is now. There is a small amount of space at the bottom, and I thought you would like to express your affection for her and save on the paper, too."

Her gaze dropped down to her newspaper as Tabitha smiled. After years of poverty and going without, of attempting to keep up appearances while they kept the debtors away from their door...

Old habits died hard. She and her mother had always sent letters together, especially as postage costs were high. Even now, with her dowry safe and secure, and their leisure time their own, her mother's instinct was to save a few pennies.

"Thank you, Mama," she said aloud. There was indeed a letter open before her, the paper covered with her mother's strong hand, which ended about three inches before the end. A quill and ink pot were beside it.

All thought of hunger forgotten, Tabitha reached for the quill and tried to organize her thoughts into something coherent. How to express what had occurred to her over the last few weeks; it was incredible to think just how much had happened since she had seen Mabel.

Why, it had been her wedding when she had first met Richard, the man she loved.

"Make haste," her mother's voice interrupted her thoughts. "Keytes is waiting for it."

Tabitha nodded and started to pour out her thoughts as best she could.

Dearest Mabel,

Just a few words from me as I close Mama's letter. I ache to see you, for I have so much to tell you that mere written words are not enough to encapsulate how I feel! The emotional journey I have been on since I saw you—I cannot express the highs! Just when I had thought all happiness may elude me, I have to admit, I have met a gentleman, and we are engaged! No mention of this to another soul, I beg you, for it is the most delightful secret. By the time you have returned, the news will be out. I cannot wait to introduce him formally, and until then, I pray you enjoy the Continent and bring back plenty of exciting stories for me.

Your loving cousin,
Tabitha

She looked carefully at her words. No, there was nothing there which could possibly give away the identity of her betrothed—and she simply had to tell someone. The secret was burning inside her, and just writing down those few words dampened the flames somewhat.

"I have finished the letter, Mama," she said quietly. "Shall I close it for you?"

Her mother was so engrossed in her newspaper that she did not even look up but nodded silently. Tabitha smiled. Her mother did love her gossip pages.

But before Tabitha had placed the letter in the envelope and sealed it, her thoughts were interrupted by a pointed question.

"Did you see?" Mrs. Chesworth held the *Bath Chronicle* and waved it at her daughter. "Did you see, Tabitha?"

Surely it was impossible for the gossips of the *ton* to have guessed...but they had disappeared from Richard's ball and were not seen for the rest of the evening.

"See what, exactly?" she managed in a croaky voice, taking her seat at the breakfast table and dropping her gaze to focus on unfolding her napkin.

Her mother's eyes were narrow when Tabitha looked back up again. "You coughed. Do you have a cough, Tabitha?"

It was so like her mother to be concerned about her health even when there was no reason to be. More importantly, if she had read something scandalous about her daughter, her mother would not have been easily distracted by a cough.

"I am quite well, Mother." She helped herself to two eggs. "Now tell me, what have you read?"

Mrs. Chesworth smoothed out the paper excitedly and passed it over. "The latest intrigue on Lord Byron!"

Tabitha glanced at the paper. There was a large marmalade stain across the page, but through the orange stickiness, she could see an outrageous headline promising all the details on page seventeen.

"It is a wonder the papers are able to keep up with him," she said dryly. "He leads an exhausting life. I am not sure whether I would have the patience."

"Oh," scolded her mother, turning back to her breakfast, "anyone with a title can do what they like, but Lord Byron is unlike anyone else, Tabitha, you must see that. Why, I heard from Mrs. Bryant the other day…"

Mrs. Chesworth's appetite for gossip frequently overwhelmed her desire for food, so Tabitha was not surprised to see her mother's teacup paused halfway to her lips as she regaled the tale.

Tabitha brushed off the marmalade with her napkin and opened the newspaper to page seventeen. There was not much to interest her—announcements of arrivals in Bath and a few engagement notices she determinedly flicked past without reading. It was while scanning for Lord Byron's name that they caught one far dearer to her: Axwick.

Her cheeks heated as her gaze raked the paragraph.

We were intrigued to note, and are pleased to announce a certain young lady, one whom few could have guessed would be walking down the aisle with her own Prince Charming, may be near her wedding day! However, we feel it is our duty to warn this young lady that her prospective groom, the dashing Duke of Axwick, is utterly bankrupt. Could he in fact be about to put the golden ring of wedlock on her fortune, rather than her finger?

Fury, hot and thick, poured through her veins. Tabitha threw down the newspaper. The runny egg yolk on her plate started to seep through the pages as her eyes were dragged, unwillingly, back to the paragraph.

Could he in fact be about to put the golden ring of wedlock on her fortune, rather than her finger?

Her mind slipped back to that heated encounter outside the Pump Room, when he had pushed her against the pillar and kissed her.

I…I am far more in your power than I thought, Tabitha. I should not—I should not have been so despicable in the Pump Room.

Tabitha laughed under her breath and turned the page. The gossips were not always right! Richard had never spoken to her about money, save that he had worked hard to ensure his brother's debts were repaid.

He is a man of honor, she reminded herself as she stared silently at her rapidly chilling breakfast, her mother's prattle continuing. A man of honor would not even consider wedding a woman for such a disgraceful reason. Had he not defended her against Mr. Lister for precisely what the *Bath Chronicle* accused him of?

Something uneasy moved in her stomach. Utterly bankrupt? Could her mother have heard something of this? She was rarely one to invite her mother to gossip, but perhaps in this case…

She was about to open her mouth to ask when she was interrupted by the jangling of a bell.

"What? The door, at this hour?" Mrs. Chesworth started. "Who could it be?"

Tabitha could hardly breathe. Could it be—it must be Richard, who else would call at such an early hour? Oh, to introduce him to her mother as her fiancé, what a surprise she would give her! *What gossip she would have to impart to her friends,* she thought dryly.

There were steps in the hallway which sounded heavy. Mutterings drifted underneath the door. How had it been so long since she had seen him? More than four and twenty hours, how had she lasted this long?

Just as she decided the exact wording to recommend him to her mother, the door opened, and Keytes stepped in—alone.

"I beg your pardon, m'lady," he intoned seriously, looking at Mrs. Chesworth, "but there is a visitor in the hallway for Miss Chesworth."

A rather awkward silence followed. Tabitha's eyes darted between her mother and their butler.

"In the hallway?" Mrs. Chesworth said rather icily. "Why does he not enter the room, or better, choose a more social hour to call?"

The butler coughed and glanced at Tabitha.

"'Tis no matter," she said hastily, rising to her feet. "I will see what this visitor wants, Mother, I do not mind the time."

Mrs. Chesworth raised an eyebrow, mirroring her daughter.

"Well, I think you should mind, Tabitha. No one of good breeding would consider nine o'clock in the morning an acceptable time to call on one's friends."

Tabitha inclined her head respectfully to her mother and tried not to run to the door. It was him, she knew it. Within seconds, she would see the man she loved.

As she shut the breakfast room door behind her, Richard turned from the looking glass.

"There you are," he said softly.

Tabitha's stomach knotted. He was, if possible, even more handsome than she had remembered. There was something else about him, too, something possessive in his look that made her want to melt right there in the hallway. His dark eyes sparkled.

It did not seem possible he was to be her husband, but he had asked her, and she had accepted. After years of waiting, after accompanying three cousins up the aisle, she would finally make the journey for herself.

Tabitha smiled. She could see the faces of the *ton's* gossips. When she was announced as the Duchess of Axwick, what would they say?

"What are you doing here," she said in mock outrage, "at such an early hour, as my mother strenuously—"

"Because it is scandalous that we have not seen each other in over a day," interrupted Richard with a knowing smile, "and I have come to rectify that mistake immediately."

Tabitha glowed with pleasure as she realized Keytes was standing in the hallway, awaiting further instruction.

"That will be all, Keytes," she said curtly, and did not open her mouth again until the door to the breakfast room had quite closed. "You cannot simply come in here and—"

All other words were stemmed by a passionate kiss. She had barely seen him move, but his strong arms were around her, claiming her, possessing her just as certainly as his lips possessed her own.

Richard finally released her.

Tabitha blinked and smiled breathlessly. "You can do whatever you want."

His eyes danced mischievously. "I thought that may be the case, and I have arrived here with the full intention to abduct you. Do you mind?"

"Mind?" Tabitha could barely think. "Abduct?"

Richard laughed and stepped back to take in her full view. "My God, but you are a pretty woman. Come on, the carriage awaits."

He bowed, and Tabitha nodded with a smile. What had she gotten herself into? Of course, she would manage to find a duke who was one of the most rebellious men she had ever met. What care did he have of the *ton*?

She grabbed the nearest pelisse and bonnet, and her reticule from the chest by the door, which Richard had flung open, letting in the cold morning. Tabitha stepped through it quickly and pulled it shut behind her, beaming at the barouche waiting for them.

Richard opened its door, his hand outstretched. "Your chariot."

Tabitha rolled her eyes as she accepted his hand, stepping up. "Why do I get the impression you are playing at asking me to run away with you?"

"Who says I am playing?" Richard pulled himself into the barouche on the other side, squashed up against her in the small carriage.

Tabitha squirmed in her seat, each inch of movement pressing her hips against him, and he groaned.

"If you are going to be so delectable," he muttered as a gentleman walked by, "then I am going to have to have you right here, right now, do you understand me?"

A thrill shot through Tabitha. To see the effect she had on a man! She had never felt more powerful...well, perhaps when she had dropped her undershift.

Her betrothed picked up the reins, and with evident skill, clicked the horses into movement.

"Are we going anywhere particular?" Tabitha asked.

He shrugged. "Wherever the road takes us, but likely outside Bath. I feel the need to escape the world, as long as you are happy to escape it with me?"

He glanced at her, and she could see genuine fear that she would not agree.

"Anywhere you go," she said quietly, moving her right hand to cover his left, "I will go."

She wanted to say more, to say how wonderful it was to see him and how, when she had woken that morning, she had been afraid the previous night and all its pleasures had been a dream. How her soul wept at the thought of waking up without him every day.

But there were not words for such a feeling, and as they turned a corner at a gentle trot, she saw Miss Priscilla Seton glance up, see her, and her mouth drop open with astonishment.

"Did you see that?" Miss Seton said to her companion, not bothering to lower her voice. "That was Miss Chesworth, and with a gentleman!"

"The Duke of Axwick!" Her companion stared. "He has never taken a young lady on a carriage ride, never!"

To be seen and recognized with him was all she wanted.

"A penny for your thoughts?"

Tabitha turned her head to see him smiling. "I beg your pardon?"

"I said, a penny for your thoughts."

She laughed. "Do you not think my thoughts are worth more?"

Now it was Richard's turn to laugh, and as they reached the open road, he chanced another look. "I barely have two coins to rub together, so it appears I will have to forego that sweet knowledge."

Tabitha joined with his laughter, but hers was hollow. Something was nagging at the back of her mind. A concern she could not pin down.

"If that were true," she said airily, "you would not own such a wonderful carriage."

I am afraid to say we do not have a carriage at present. But I will ask Matthews to call one for you, and you may take your pick of any pelisse or greatcoat I can offer you.

Why had Lady Charlotte spoken such a falsehood?

Richard shook his head as they sped up, turning a corner, and Tabitha was forced to raise her hand to her bonnet.

"'Tis not mine. I have borrowed it from a friend—William Lennox, are you acquainted with him?"

Tabitha's heart sank. It was not his carriage. It was borrowed finery, her mother would call it. Ignoring his question as they passed the last inn in Bath and started to enter the countryside, she said quietly, "I did not realize you had been forced to part with so much to cover your brother's debts, leaving you with so little."

Richard shrugged. "'Tis no matter. It was my duty as an Axwick to ensure the family honor was retained. Besides, you have enough for the both of us!"

He certainly did not seem particularly concerned about his lack of fortune, but now she came to think about it, the only expense she had ever seen him make was for the ball, and was that not for Lady Charlotte's benefit?

It was a relief when the barouche, freed from the confines of the city, slowed once more, for otherwise the motion may have made Tabitha quite sick.

She had to say something. She could not permit this fear to continue unchecked.

"Richard," she began, but was halted immediately by one simple movement. He placed a hand on her knee and squeezed it gently.

The nausea turned to butterflies in her stomach. She loved him so much, and he cared for her. She was merely discovering his sense of humor, that must be it. There was much to learn about him, for he was a complicated man.

The barouche glided slowly down the country lane, and Richard leaned back, relaxing the reins and allowing the horses to fall into a natural trot.

"How long do you and your mother plan to stay in Bath? For the season?"

Tabitha smiled. Here was additional proof he did truly care about her, for how could you plan a wedding unless you discussed the planned movements of your future spouse?

"We had not set a date," she replied. "Perhaps another four weeks?"

"And where do you plan on going next?" Richard's hand was still on her knee, and he smiled devilishly. "Perhaps you could come straight to Stonehaven Lacey?"

Tabitha's heart leapt. "Will…will there be enough time for the preparations by then? Four weeks seems hardly sufficient."

Unbidden, her mind became flooded with visions for their wedding: the church adorned with her favorite flowers, white and red roses, candles flickering in the spring breeze, and Richard waiting for her.

She was awoken from her reverie by another of Richard's shrugs.

"I am almost sure I can have it arranged by then," he said softly, his hand moving to enclose hers. "If not, the most important thing is that we are together."

Tabitha swelled with love. "I wonder what my mother will do after that."

"I am sure she will find something to do in London," he said dismissively. "Now, is it down here?"

Tabitha looked down the two lanes. They looked identical. "And where shall we live?"

"Live?" he looked at her, distracted, and then smiled. "Let's go left."

"Live," she prompted him. Was there anything better than sitting with your betrothed in an open carriage, trotting down the Bath countryside lanes, discussing the life that you were going to lead once you were wed?

Richard grinned. "Well, I will probably be living in Stonehaven Lacey. I am sure we can find you some sort of lodgings in the village, if you would like to be near me. You will have to pay for it, of course."

Tabitha laughed. "You surely cannot be in that sort of financial difficulty."

As soon as the words were out of her mouth, she regretted them. A shadow clouded his eyes, and he looked away and cast his eyes on the winding lane ahead of them. Silence fell, and the awkwardness seemed to creep over the back of her neck.

"I am sorry," she said finally. "You do not like talking about money, do you?"

It took him a little while to answer. "No. Since I gained my majority, money has been a source only of pain and irritation. There is no good in it."

Tabitha bit her lip. She had no wish to force the topic on him, but if they were to be married, should they not be able to have this conversation? It would hardly do for something so critical to be off limits between them.

"You said that...your brother left many debts."

The carriage sped up as Richard touched the horses with the whip. The bare branches of the trees moved over them in a gentle breeze, creaking in the wind.

She swallowed. "But that you have paid them—"

"Almost paid them," growled Richard. "Do we have to speak about this, is there not any other topic that would entertain you?"

"If we are to live together—" Tabitha began, but she was cut off immediately.

"When I come to live with a woman," said Richard with a grin and a wink, "and who knows when that day will come, then I will talk more about my financial situation. 'Tis not seemly, after all, to speak of such things with a young, unmarried woman."

Tabitha opened her mouth but then closed it again. He was right; until they were married, it was none of her concern.

"What I am more interested in," he said, "is when I can see you again."

Tabitha raised an eyebrow and squeezed his hand. "You are seeing me right now."

"You know what I mean," he growled, a grin on his face. "Tabitha, I swear…I had never experienced anything like that. Never."

A flush of pleasure tinged her cheeks. "You are the world's most impressive flatterer, Axwick."

Richard groaned. "Back to Axwick? Ye gods, what could I have possibly done to deserve such a punishment?"

Tabitha laughed. "I just like to keep you on your toes, that is all. I cannot have you grow too complacent, can I?"

The carriage turned another corner, and they joined the Bath road again. "I did not have much of a chance with you, did I?"

"What do you mean?" A crease appeared in Tabitha's forehead. "If I remember rightly, *your grace*," causing Richard to groan, "'twas you who chased me."

"Me!" With a sudden jolt, he picked up the reins and brought the horses to a complete stop. "I think you have misremembered, my lady."

He turned to look at her, and Tabitha saw with pleasure that his mock glare was paired with desire. He wanted her. It made her feel alive.

"I am almost sure," she said in a stern voice, "that I was the one who walked away from you at Lady Romeril's ball—and outside the Pump Rooms."

Richard was leaning forward now. Tabitha's heart was pounding, desperately wanting—what?

"And did you not come to your ball dressed in all your finery, hoping to catch a particular duke?"

Tabitha had been conscious of the way her body was growing warmer, but she stopped at his words. "My ball?"

Richard froze. "What?"

She could not have misheard him. "Richard, you said my ball. I have not thrown a ball, what do you mean?"

His mouth opened and then closed.

Ice slipped into her heart. "You...you have just mistaken me for one of the other young ladies that you have courted and bedded, haven't you?"

"No!" Richard said hastily. "No, I—"

"I knew I was not the first, but to be mistaken for another," said Tabitha wretchedly, tugging her hands free of his.

"You have misunderstood me. I arranged the ball—"

"Please, take me back." Tabitha sat upright and turned to face the front of the carriage, quite ignoring the slumped head of her companion. To think that she had considered herself so special, so unique in his affects. He had used all these tricks before. Would she ever get used to that?

She had been the only one that he had proposed marriage to, the only one that he had danced with in the last three years. If that did not mean something, then what did?

The carriage had stopped again. She could sense his gaze on her but looked away.

"I held the ball for you."

The words were so quiet, she was not entirely sure he had spoken, until she glanced at him and saw the concern in his eyes. "What ball?"

Richard swallowed. He looked uncomfortable but resolved. "You only returned to Bath that morning and found the invitation. You thought that it was just a ball I had decided to host, an excuse for dancing. But in truth, it was for you."

"What do you mean?" she breathed.

He sighed heavily. "I am a duke, Tabitha. I have never had to work so hard to impress a young lady in my life as I have with you. But there was a moment when I was unsure if I could win you—and I had to do anything it would take."

Tabitha flushed and shifted in her seat.

"I wanted to see you, to have more time with you, to impress you." Richard cleared his throat. "And so, I threw a ball. Without you, there would have been no ball."

Tabitha stared at him. It did not seem possible—with all their financial difficulties, to host a lavish party in the middle of the Bath season…why?

"But I almost did not attend."

Richard laughed. "I know! Charlotte warned me that you would not be impressed by such things. I needed you in my house. I cared not for the other guests. I waited in the hall for an hour—if you had not shown up, I would have abandoned everyone and gone to my study for the rest of the evening."

Tabitha wanted to express her gratitude, her shock at being honored in such a way, but she did not have the words.

She did not need words. With only a little hesitation, she reached forward and pulled Richard to her by the lapels of his greatcoat. His arms quickly tightened around her waist as she kissed him.

Every inch of her body craved Richard's touch. It was a cruel fate that they were sitting in a carriage where anyone could come across them. As the kiss deepened, she moaned in pleasure. Eventually, the kiss ended.

"I should take you back," he said. "Are you quite recovered now?"

Tabitha laughed shakily. "I do not think I shall ever recover."

CHAPTER FOURTEEN

IT WAS WITH great personal satisfaction that Richard placed the final banknote on the desk.

"There," he said, leaning back with satisfaction. "The last of it."

He could hardly believe it. His eyes lingered on the money. It represented so much: years of hard work, dedication, and personal sacrifice. Now that the last had been handed over, a huge weight had been lifted from his shoulders.

"Are you quite well?" a dry voice asked.

Richard looked up to see his accountant, Mr. Birch's, eyebrows raised. He was an older gentleman, but the Axwickes had always kept a Birch as an accountant, and he was not going to be the one who altered that tradition.

"I am very well," he said calmly. "But I must admit, even *I* thought I would never see the end of my family's debts. It feels like a miracle."

"Really? When I review your accounts, your grace, it feels like no miracle at all."

Richard shrugged. "Well, perhaps not. We have certainly scrimped and saved, and mortgaged a small part of the land in Rutland."

"And used Lady Charlotte's dowry," Birch added, "if I am not mistaken."

There was no judgment in his tone, but Richard bristled. Did this man think he would have done so if there had been any other choice?

"Yes," he conceded, shifting in the leather seat. "But I hope to see that restored, just as I intend one day to repay the mortgage on the land. But a mortgage to a bank is utterly preferable to a debt to a cardsharp, as I am sure you can appreciate."

Mr. Birch said nothing but stared silently at Richard. It was this passionless quality which had made generations of Birches excellent choices for accountants, but it did not endear the current man to the duke.

"Well, 'tis done," said Richard, more snappish than he had intended. "Lady Charlotte and I can rest easy now."

Mr. Birch looked as though he was going to say something. He leaned forward, eyes fixed firmly on Richard. But he thought better of it, and picking up the banknotes from the desk, carefully counting them and entered the numbers onto a neat ledger his assistant had offered him as soon as Richard had entered the room.

"And 'tis done," echoed Mr. Birch. "Your grace, I am grateful and honored to be the one to tell you that the whole forty-two thousand pounds is indeed paid in full."

"'Tis a king's ransom," he muttered aloud.

Mr. Birch nodded. "I cannot quite believe how such a debt was ever created."

"And it is no concern of yours," Richard said coldly, hopefully reminding the man of his place. "So, I suggest you keep any speculation to yourself, Birch, for you have no grounds for it."

Mr. Birch frowned as he said in a serious tone, "Of course, your grace. I would advise, however, that before you consider repaying the mortgage on Stonehaven Lacey in Rutland, you give due consideration to the dowry of Lady Charlotte."

Richard did not speak immediately, but felt the familiar painful tug at his heartstrings. Few would have made the decision he did, and sometimes...

"I will undoubtedly regret it at some point," he admitted gruffly. "But Charlotte has never shown any interest toward marriage before, and she is past thirty, almost five and thirty. She spends more time as a chaperone to the younger generation rather than dancing herself."

"And she was…amenable to such a sacrifice?"

Mr. Birch's question was impertinent and he seemed to realize this, his gaze dropping to his ledger.

"Lady Charlotte recognizes sacrifices have to be made," Richard said. "She is a St. Maur. She would do whatever necessary to ensure the continued success of this family, as would I. As it happens, it appears the dowry would never have been needed."

"And so, the Axwick line is currently without an heir," Mr. Birch said delicately. "For if it is true that Lady Charlotte will not marry, and you are currently unmarried…"

Something wrenched at Richard's stomach. Yes, he had been forced to accept that the Axwick title would go to a lesser branch of the family, the Winslows. It had been a difficult decision, but he did not regret it. The Axwick estate was intact. He had not been the one to destroy it.

A small, golden clock on the mantle chimed thrice in the silence between them, and Richard rose. He had only intended to spend a few minutes with Mr. Birch. Visiting hours were coming to an end, and he had one other visit to make before they did.

A rush of excitement filled his heart. He was going to see Tabitha for the first time in two days. Staying away from her had been necessary to prevent raising suspicion in the gossips of Bath. He had heard from his sister that Tabitha had returned home in a hired carriage, which was all to the good, but he was unsure whether Mrs. Chesworth was aware her daughter had returned home the day after the ball.

If he wanted to continue enjoying pleasure with Miss Tabitha Chesworth, it was essential her mother had no inkling of what was happening. Every hour away from her had been sweet torture, and he could not wait to see her.

Mr. Birch had also risen, and he inclined his head to the duke. "Well, I hope you are right about Lady Charlotte's dowry, your grace. You never know when a young lady takes it into her head to get married."

Richard laughed and shook his head. "No, you do not."

"Why, just this morning," said Mr. Birch, walking around his desk to open the door for Richard, "a young lady came to see me–a very wealthy young lady–to make some changes to her fortune, for she is to be married. To tell the truth, she is a young lady which the tittle tattle pages of Bath would be most intrigued to see walk up the aisle."

"Marriage is more like a march into the jaws of death," said Richard wryly as they walked along the corridor. "It is certainly off the cards for me, if I were to be a gambling man, until I find a woman it is impossible to live without. 'Tis hard to see such a day."

They had reached the front door but instead of opening it, Mr. Birch stopped in his tracks and stared at Richard in utter bewilderment. The look of confusion deepened, but the accountant coughed past the embarrassing silence.

"'Tis none of my business, I am sure," he said gruffly. "Thank you for your visit today, your grace, and I hope you do not take offence when I say I hope I do not see you for many months."

Richard smiled, a little confused by the odd behavior of Mr. Birch, but inclined his head politely and stepped out into the wintery air.

He took a deep breath, allowing his lungs to fill with the biting cold. He had been a drowning man and had finally reached the surface of the water, so sweet was that breath. There was nothing comparable to finally, after three years of worry, penny-pinching, and sacrifice, to officially be able to say the only debt the dukedom of Axwick had was to the bank.

Hell, in five years, perhaps, if the harvests were good and some long-term investments finally came through, even that debt could be gone.

He could never have believed it when his brother had died, when his brother Arnold's debts poured into the sinking ship that was the house of Axwick, that it was even possible to be here today. Yet, here he stood, safe in the knowledge nothing could harm him again. They had done it, he and Charlotte. Their mother, God love her, would have been proud.

"A bite to eat, sir?" A street seller, haggard with few teeth, had crept up and thrust a pie that looked a good five days old, toward him. "Keep you warm this bitter afternoon?"

"No, the gentleman wants ale, do you not, sir?" Another appeared, a man with a long, straggly beard and watery eyes, holding out a sign pointing to an alehouse down the road. "Ale to warm your heart, and perhaps a girl to warm your bed?"

"I want neither pie, ale, or a girl," said Richard, barely able to hide his grin. "Now be off with you, or I shall call the River Police."

They scrambled away, and Richard set off with a clear purpose to the south of the city, where Tabitha and her mother had taken lodgings. It had not been difficult to find their address, and though Charlotte had frowned, her disapproval had not dampened his spirits— or his need to be with her.

Tabitha. She stayed on his mind. Even his conversation with Mr. Birch had been tediously long, for each moment with him was time he was not with her.

Richard knocked into a gentleman walking in the opposite direction.

"Mind where you are going, sir!" The gentleman stared at him in disbelief. "Take a care, sir, take a care!"

But Richard barely heard him. He was on Tabitha's street, and words circled his mind as he attempted to choose the most delightful thing he could say to her.

When he rapped on the door and was welcomed in by the butler, he was shown into the drawing room occupied not by Tabitha, but her mother.

Mrs. Chesworth rose with a smile and curtsied. "Your grace."

Richard stared, open mouthed. He had been so certain Tabitha would be at home. Now he saw Mrs. Chesworth, he could see the strong resemblance between the two of them. It was clear Mrs. Chesworth had been a beautiful woman, and in truth, she still held that beauty in a subdued way.

Richard realized his mouth was still open. Overcoming his surprise and disappointment, he smiled.

"My dear, Mrs. Chesworth," he said with a deep bow. "I had been hoping to make your acquaintance, and I admit I simply could not wait for a more formal, public occasion. Can you possibly find it in your heart to forgive my intrusion?"

He had always been able to charm women. Mrs. Chesworth blushed at his words, but he could see she was flattered.

"Your grace, you are always welcome in this house," she said, indicating he was to be seated. "I am just sorry we have not yet had the pleasure of your company. I enter into public very little these days, and I am most glad you have not awaited that opportunity, for I fear you would have been waiting too long."

Richard seated himself and smiled. "And yet you deprive the rest of society of your presence? I simply cannot understand it, Mrs. Chesworth. Unless you do so to allow those of us privileged to be called your friends the absolute best of your presence. Say it is so, and most importantly, name me as one of those friends, and you shall be forgiven."

Mrs. Chesworth smiled graciously. "Now you are a flatterer, your grace, and I shall pass your apologies along to my daughter, whom I suspect you truly came to call on?"

Her smile was so similar to her daughter's that Richard was momentarily dumbstruck.

She laughed. "Oh, your grace, I have lived longer in the world than you, and I am well accustomed to the charming ways of the nobility. Do not concern yourself, I am very flattered you thought to even charm me at all!"

"You are a delight, Mrs. Chesworth, and I hope to know you better."

She reached to pull the bell. "I am sure you shall. The apologies of my daughter must be given, your grace, but I hope she will be back soon. She went out this morning to see her accountant–she was always much better with numbers than I. She is also visiting Miss Worsley, where she will be dining this evening. You are, of course, very welcome to stay to dine with me and await her return?"

Richard did not hear a word after Mrs. Chesworth uttered 'accountant'. Tabitha had visited an accountant that morning–that very morning.

Something bitter rose in his throat, and his pulse quickened in panic. He had thought nothing of Birch's words but now they seemed vitally important. A young lady to be married–and most importantly, one the gossips of the *ton* would be intrigued, surprised even, to see walk up the aisle.

Even he had heard the joking laughter about Miss Tabitha Chesworth, three times a bridesmaid and never a bride.

Could it be possible Tabitha was in fact engaged to another gentleman? Could she have kept such a secret from him, a gentleman she had given herself to so willingly?

"...as well as numbers, she is a very talented linguist," Mrs. Chesworth was saying, not having noticed his sudden shock. "She speaks French very well, and a smattering of Italian, and the Latin she learned never left her. I say the governess was well worth it–although of course, we use Latin very little these days..."

Mrs. Chesworth obviously wanted to ensure her daughter's accomplishments were noted by him, but Richard could barely concentrate on her words.

Tabitha, engaged? She belonged to another man. Could this be true?

"Do you want to get married, one day?" he had asked her.

And she had replied, *"Yes. Yes I do."*

Richard shook his head slightly as though to rid it of water. No, he could not think this way. Why would Tabitha allow him to woo her, to court her, to dance with her, to steal kisses, to act as though she wanted his love, if all that time she had secretly been engaged to another?

And it certainly was a secret, for her mother was obviously unaware.

"–her beauty has been noted for it," she was saying.

No, if Mrs. Chesworth had any inkling her daughter was engaged to be married, she would hardly be saying such things to him, encouraging him to see her daughter as a potential suit.

Seated on the uncomfortable chaise longue and forced to hear the prattlings of Tabitha's mother, a thought crossed Richard's mind that felt like ice.

Perhaps the answer was more simple. Perhaps Tabitha did not care. Perhaps she liked the thrill of the chase, of being desired, of being pursued. Perhaps she gained a thrill from his pathetic attentions.

Eventually she had given in to him, and she may even have enjoyed it–and what did it matter? Any child from such an encounter could surely be explained away, blamed on her other lover, whoever this man was.

Richard found himself full of fury and jealousy for this unnamed man who Tabitha clearly loved more than him. She would marry another, and doubtless laugh at him for being so vulnerable, so stupid to think any word from her mouth was true.

"But then as I told her, she would always look good in white." Mrs. Chesworth was completely oblivious to the torture Richard was undergoing, speaking on with a bright smile. "Few young ladies do, your grace, but Tabitha is radiantly beautiful…"

She was radiantly beautiful, and he had been taken in. Utterly and completely taken in. He, the sixteenth Duke of Axwick. He had never thought it possible.

"That is one of hers, there," Mrs. Chesworth pointed at a still-life painting hanging on the wall. "Her master told her…"

Richard tried to nod and smile as anger burned through him. His stomach cringed as though someone had thrown a punch at him, so intense was the thought that next occurred to him.

Perhaps Tabitha, despite all she had said about her father, was of a gambling nature after all. Maybe she had found some young pup to propose marriage to her, but she was trying her luck with him, too— and gambling on the fact that she may be with child.

If she was not, she could go back to her other gentleman. She would be married, which is what she wanted.

If she was with child, however, she would tell him, and of course he would have provided for her, provided for the child, perhaps even married her.

And she would become a duchess.

Richard's eyes darkened as he sat helplessly listening to Tabitha's mother. How could he ever have been so stupid to think she had cared for him?

CHAPTER FIFTEEN

"THANK YOU, KEYTES." Tabitha stepped into the hallway and shivered as the warmth of her home sank in. "It is freezing out there, and I think in hindsight, I should have asked Miss Worsley to call me a carriage. Walking back has–"

A voice stopped her in her tracks. Instead of her mother's lilting tones, the drawing room door was slightly ajar, allowing a deep, male voice to seep into the hallway. It was familiar.

Handing the butler her pelisse and bonnet and placing her reticule on the table, she moved quietly toward the door. The man's voice grew louder and clearer.

"...again about the painting, Mrs. Chesworth, I do not recall if–"

"Ah, she was very young when she completed it, your grace. In fact, her art tutor, Mr. Griffins, told me himself, if it had not been for–"

A heat of joy washed over Tabitha as she recognized the voice. It was Richard.

This was it, then... The perfect opportunity for her to introduce him, the man she loved, to her mother as her fiancé. Was there a better time to share the news which would make her mother so happy?

But Richard had asked her to keep it a secret...

"I was thinking that we must agree not to tell anyone about this. It must be a secret, you understand, a secret between us. You and me."

But surely not from her own mother! It had been difficult enough not telling Lady Charlotte, and she had been sorely tempted–not just to share the news but to explain her undoubtedly odd appearance in her library the morning after the ball!

Tabitha took a deep breath and placed her hand on the cold door handle. This was it. She was about to see her betrothed and share the happy news with her mother.

She opened the door and took a few steps into the room, her gaze immediately drawn to the handsome gentleman sitting rather awkwardly at one end of the chaise longue.

Her heart fluttered. Just seeing Richard St. Maur was enough to fill her with so much joy, she was surprised it kept beating. But he did not look happy–perhaps because he had been forced to endure, in her absence, her mother's nonsense about her adequate painting.

"Ah, Tabitha," her mother smiled, her eyes wide and expressive. "The duke here has kindly been keeping me company, and I must say, you are earlier than I had expected. Did Miss Worsley not invite you to stay for dinner after all?"

"Miss Worsley had an urgent engagement to attend, and I was unable to stay."

She had spoken every word while looking at Richard, but he had not looked at her. Indeed, he had turned slightly away from her as she entered the room. Perhaps if he caught her eye, they would be unable to hide their feelings from her mother.

"Ah, well, that is disappointing," her mother said. "But it is good you were able to see her at all. Did you hear, your grace–"

"Mother," Tabitha interrupted with a smile, taking a few steps toward Richard. "I am so glad you have had the chance to meet the Duke of Axwick, because...well, you see, the Duke and I are–"

"Going for a walk," he finished for her.

Tabitha blinked in surprise as Richard stood hastily.

"Are we not, Miss Chesworth?" He glared with such fierceness, the kind she had seen when she had first met him. His presence overpowered her, and she found herself nodding. "It is such a lovely afternoon,

Mrs. Chesworth, we thought we would take a walk around the Sydney Gardens. That is, unless you object?"

Tabitha said nothing as her mother spluttered her enthusiastic permission. He was still staring at her, as though he was attempting to tell her something without using words. Something hot was spiraling in her stomach as wild thoughts of kissing against a tree in a secluded part of the gardens swept into Tabitha's mind.

"Thank you, Mother," she said quickly. "We will not be long, of course."

"Just be careful of..."

But before her mother could finish her sentence, Richard had bowed and strode out of the room. Tabitha smiled at the wildness of the man she loved.

"We will not be long," she promised her mother again before hurriedly following the duke out of the room. He was already standing at the front door, waiting for her.

She stepped through the doorway, pushing against him and smiling as her breasts brushed against his chest. As soon as she was outside, he slammed the door behind them.

It was a short walk to the park. Tabitha hoped they would linger, prolonging the time they had together, but Richard was striding so quickly, she had to run to keep up with him.

"I have missed you," she said in a low tone. "Why–"

"The weather is indeed cold," he said in a dull voice as a pair of ladies passed them.

Tabitha blushed. It was best to keep such words of love to herself. They were in public, and it would not do for the gossips of Bath to guess their secret engagement.

But her emotions had been awoken by him–and far more than her emotions–and she simply had to pour some of them out of herself, even if it meant discovery. What harm could it do?

"It seems like forever," she murmured as they passed under the garden gates, "since I last saw you."

He nodded but said nothing, eyes fixed ahead of them.

Tabitha licked her lips nervously. "And you...you have been well since then?"

Richard grunted. Now she considered him more closely, he looked sullen or angry. But this was not anger, precisely. It was something more.

A flicker of concern entered Tabitha's heart.

Was it possible, despite all of her hopes, that he was going to change his mind and not marry her? The very thought was painful. Could he regret making love to her? Could he be worried that she was with child? He had forgone the hope of fatherhood for so long. Was he terrified at the very thought of it?

They walked for several minutes in complete silence and without passing a single person.

Then Tabitha grabbed at his arm and brought Richard to a halt. "Is there something on your mind?"

They stood there, a mere foot apart, and still he would not look her in the eyes. "No."

"Yet, you are quiet," Tabitha said softly. "Why?"

Richard shrugged. "No reason. A man may be quiet if he wants to be."

He was prickly.

A wintery breeze brushed through the gardens, and Tabitha shivered. The sunlight was fading, and they could not stay long without a chaperone. But this was her time with him, and she would not waste it.

Smiling, she took his hand in hers and squeezed it. He did not return the act of affection, but he did finally look her in the eyes–and Tabitha was surprised to see not love but something bordering on irritation.

"You know," she said quietly, taking a small step toward him and trying to ignore the desire to just kiss him. "I have found my bed rather empty without you in it."

She thought her words would warm his spirits, but something strange flickered across his face–something akin to...jealousy.

"We have only made love," he snapped, wrenching his hand from hers. "If you miss the feeling of a man beside you, you must be accustomed to sharing it with someone else."

Tabitha stared at him in horror. "Someone–someone else?"

It had to be a joke–a bad one, made in poor taste. But he glared, and the fire in his eyes had no warmth like before. Where there had once been desire, there was only bitterness.

"How could you possibly think that of me?"

CHAPTER SIXTEEN

RICHARD HAD NEVER before understood the expression *to make one's blood boil*. He could feel it frothing in his veins, pounding in his ears, and throbbing in his chest.

He stared at Tabitha. She looked surprised to be told of her treachery.

"How can you say that?" she repeated, her arms listlessly at her sides.

His fingers felt as though they were on fire. It was not purely anger but pain, too.

How could he have allowed himself to get into this blasted position? How could he have opened up after years of bedding women without any thought to consequences–after vowing never to get emotionally involved, to avoid marriage, to ensure the family line was not to continue?

"I said it," he growled through gritted teeth as a couple passed them arm in arm, "because you are engaged to another, Tabitha–no, do not deny it! You have been playing with me, playing like a dog plays with a toy. Seeing what I will say, what I will do, how much I will declare to you…"

Richard's voice trailed off as pain overcame him. The woman who had caused so much agony was staring, eyes wide. It did naught but increase her beauty, and a stab of shame hit his stomach that he could have been so weak, so easily taken in.

"H-how could you?" Tabitha spluttered, trying to collect herself before speaking. "How could you possibly think that?"

"I will tell you what I think," he muttered. "I think you have been lying from the beginning. I think you were already engaged to this other gentleman, whoever he is, and you just…just wanted to play up to the idea you had been passed over by other gentlemen. This always a bridesmaid nonsense…I should have seen through it immediately."

"Play up to the idea?" She looked utterly shocked. "What are you talking about, Richard?"

Her words tore into his heart like ice, and Richard actually took a step back, unable to be close to her.

"Richard, I do not understand," she said. "Has someone told you something of me–something false that I can explain?"

Richard shook his head, dark hair falling over his eyes, and he brushed it away irritably.

A gentleman passed them, nodding politely to Richard who merely scowled back. What right did anyone else have to be here, in his private hell?

Someone's hand was on his arm pulling him off the path and toward some trees. It was Tabitha.

"What the–"

"Come with me," she said firmly. After taking a few more strides, making sure they were hidden from the path, Tabitha rounded on him with a frown. "Now then, Richard St. Maur, it is my turn to speak. You have said naught but wild accusations of myself and another gentleman–which is complete nonsense–and I have only ever told you the truth. I am not engaged to another, and I never have been."

Richard stared. Her eyes were bright, but every word out of those delectable lips sounded like lies. How could he trust her, knowing she had been to Mr. Birch to prepare for a husband?

"Someone," he said in a slightly strangled voice, "someone of good standing has told me you were engaged to another."

It was Tabitha's turn to take a shocked step back. Her hand fluttered to her chest, and she whispered, "Engaged to another?"

Richard nodded curtly and glanced at the path. There was no point standing here, like two lovers hoping for a secretive stolen kiss. He had never felt more alone, even with Tabitha right before him.

"But that is not true," she said and she reached out to take his face in her hands. It hurt to see them, the same eyes that had caught his when he had made love to her. "Who told you this?"

Richard opened his mouth to answer but hesitated.

"Why, just this morning, a young lady came to see me–a very wealthy young lady–to make some changes to her fortune, for she is to be married. To tell the truth, she is a young lady which the tittle tattle pages of Bath would be most intrigued to see walk up the aisle."

Now he came to think about it, Birch had never actually stated the young woman's name. Bath was not a large place, to be sure, but it was certainly possible there was more than one young lady of fortune who had visited an accountant that morning.

Richard hardened his resolve. No, Birch could have meant no other. You had to be deaf and blind not to hear the jokes about Miss Tabitha Chesworth.

"It was my accountant, Mr. Birch," he said curtly. "I saw him this afternoon on a matter of business, and he intimated to me that a young woman would be getting married."

Tabitha laughed. "And you took that, of course, to mean that I was engaged to another man?"

"I do not have this conversation for my own pleasure," retorted Richard, hands flexing with frustration. The night was drawing in, but he had never felt so unbearably hot in all his life. "He said the gossips of Bath would be most interested to see that young lady walk up the aisle."

The words echoed around the glade of trees, and all the fight disappeared from Tabitha's body. Her shoulders slumped, and her gaze finally dropped to the mud beneath their feet.

The temptation to ignore all his fears, to ignore the words of Birch, to ignore all his instincts, almost took over. By God, what he would give to wash away the last few hours of knowledge and take Tabitha in his arms and...

"And that is all?" Tabitha asked. "Is my notoriety as a young lady no one would like to marry enough to convince you that someone else must wish to?"

Richard would not back down. "You were that woman," he said with more certainty than he felt. "I have no doubt of that, Tabitha."

She laughed again, but it was a derisive laugh that cut him. "Because you are able to see all things? You may be a duke, but that does not make you omniscient!"

"Because your mother told me today you had gone to your accountant this morning."

She stared as though he had gone completely mad, and Richard wondered if he had. What had he come to, standing in a public park and hissing accusations at a young woman who could have done nothing wrong? How could he say such things to the woman he regarded as the greatest person he had ever met?

Tabitha raised her hands in mock surrender. "You are a complete fool."

Richard opened his mouth to retort but could think of nothing to say.

Her breath billowed out in the cold air. "Richard, I did go to see my accountant this morning, and that accountant was Mr. Birch, and it...it was in preparation for marriage and–"

"Aha–I knew it, I knew I should have trusted my instincts!" he said, thrusting an accusatory finger in her face. "I knew you were engaged to another."

"If you would let me finish." She glared at him with such ferocity, he felt slightly cowed. "Oh, Richard. I do love you, and I can see our life together is going to be far more exhausting and exhilarating than I had first supposed."

Richard's mind, frazzled with fear and hope and jealousy, took a little while to fully understand her words.

"The marriage I was preparing for with Mr. Birch was our own."

A bolt of lightning overhead would have been nothing compared to the shock ricocheting through his body.

Their marriage?

But they were not engaged to be married. He had never even considered making such an offer. In the future, perhaps, after a few years of trust and understanding, but now? How in God's name could she think such a thing?

When did she even think a proposal had been made?

"You see?" Tabitha said quietly, taking his hands and squeezing them. "Oh, Richard, to see you jealous over yourself...once I had understood, it was quite amusing. My love, there is no one else, only you. My betrothed. In a few months, my husband."

"My betrothed. In a few months, my husband."

The words echoed around Richard's mind like a gunshot, and it dawned on him.

He had to tell her. He had to explain this terrible mistake. How it had been made, he had no idea. How he could have possibly prevented it, he could not tell. But despite Tabitha clearly wishing it, they were not engaged.

Richard swallowed. This was not the conversation he had expected to have. If he did not say something...

"Tabitha," he said quietly. "We are not engaged."

CHAPTER SEVENTEEN

SHE STARED HIM. The man she loved–the man she had given everything, absolutely everything to.

All the sound in the Sydney Gardens—the carriages trundling by on the nearest street, the horses neighing in the cold winter evening air, the people talking on the path, the laughter of revelers making their way to their evening entertainment... It all faded into nothingness.

The world was without sound and without color. All she could see was Richard, tall and brooding, face contorted with confusion. All she could hear were his last words.

We are not engaged.

Only the biting evening air reminded her that this was not some sort of fantastical nightmare, but her real life.

"We are," she said eventually, her eyes not leaving his. "We are engaged, Richard."

He laughed bitterly and shook his head. "Tabitha, I think I would certainly know if we were engaged. You are going to have to trust me when I say we are not."

She shook her head, as though she could rid her mind of his words. This could not be happening–this was a mistake, a misunderstanding. All she had to do was explain everything, and he would recall his proposal...short though it had been.

"You asked me," she said quietly, "in the library. You asked me, and I said yes, while we were…"

Tabitha felt her cheeks flush at exactly what they had been doing when he had made that offer, his hands on her breasts, his lips on her neck–well, it was no wonder he did not remember saying those exact words.

"While we were kissing, Richard."

She had not expected him to be embarrassed. Waving his hand as though batting away her words, Richard shook his head.

"As glorious as that moment was, Tabitha, I did not lose my head sufficiently to offer marriage when I certainly was not considering doing so," he said seriously. "You knew my offer."

Tabitha stared in disbelief. She would not have made this up, she could not have fabricated such an offer. What had Richard said, what were his exact words?

She closed her eyes. She had had one leg wrapped around him, the spines of the books digging into her back and forcing her closer to him, closer than she had ever been, and she had glorified in it, loved it, loved the feeling of his fingers brushing past her nipples, loved the kisses that deepened and deepened as she moaned into his mouth…

Tabitha, will you make me very happy?

"You said," she spoke slowly, opening her eyes to gaze into his own. "You said Tabitha, will you make me very happy? And I said yes."

Richard's face darkened.

"Tabitha, that was about my offer. My offer to seduce you. To make both of us happy–to bring both of us pleasure. It was just about that night."

Her mouth fell open in horror. No–no this could not be. There was no possible way she could have misunderstood, surely?

"It was just about that night," she repeated in a hollow voice. "Just about the pleasure. Not about me?"

"Now, I did not say that," Richard said hastily. "I do not mean that,

Tabitha, I–"

"And there they are, your true colors," she said bitterly, taking a step away from him. "I knew they would come out eventually and your true intentions would be revealed. All you wanted was my body."

"No, I–"

"I wish I had been strong enough to withstand you long enough to discover it for myself," she said, every word pouring out of her like bile, purging the hurt and the pain from her, because she had never felt pain like this. "I suppose I am lucky you have only had two sordid encounters from me."

She could not face him. As he reached out and tried to take her hand, she pulled away. "Were all your stories about your father and brother even true? All those sorrowful tales about debts and gambling, or had you perhaps heard about my father? Did you create that story to get close to me, *your grace*, was that all part of the plan?"

She had been so foolish, so easily flattered into giving herself up. The perfect story to gain her affections.

Shame, embarrassment, pride—they all rushed through her. Tabitha turned away, unable to think, desperately attempting to hold back tears.

How could this have happened? Discovering the man she loved, and she did love him, had absolutely no desire to be with her?

She did not know Richard St. Maur, sixteenth Duke of Axwick, at all.

"I am one in a long line of ladies," she said, "who has been taken in with your words and kisses."

She wanted to walk away from him but did not have the strength. She could barely stand. If she took another step, then she would collapse under the weight of her tears.

"Tabitha..." He grabbed her arm and turned her to face him. "Every word I said to you was true, I swear it, and not just about my father and brother, but about my vow. I just do not wish to wed."

Tabitha tried to pull away, but he had a firm grip.

"I have never hidden that from you," he said sharply. "'Twas never a secret, my desire to remain a bachelor. I have not lied to you–"

"Ah, but you did not need to, you got what you wanted without lies," she shot back, tears prickling in the corners of her eyes. "You just wanted to…to make love to me, your grace, and now that you have, I cannot understand why you bothered to see me again."

He snorted at her. "If I had just wanted to make love, I could have gone to half a dozen women in London or Bath where I am welcomed for such…" His eyes widened with horror as he heard the words that came out of his mouth. "I did not mean it…"

"I understand," she said dully, wrenching her arm from his. "I just did not realize I knew you so little. That I meant that little."

The truth hurt her so much. She had to find a way to walk away from him, to preserve her dignity.

"Am I one of *that* number now?" she whispered. "Just a tart you can have your way with whenever you choose?"

Richard shook his head vigorously—looking as guilty as sin. "You mean everything…"

"I cannot believe you." What could he possibly say after breaking her heart? "I am used goods, and there is no point attempting to convince me otherwise. But I am even more disgusted with you."

He held her gaze, looking wretched.

"How could you have allowed this to happen? After all the jokes and the laughter of the *ton,* always the bridesmaid and never the bride, after all of that–you have condemned me, your grace. I will never marry. No one will touch me now."

She wanted to make him feel what she felt, standing here in the cold and dark with all hope for the future wrenched away from her.

He was staring as though he had never seen her before. Perhaps he never had. Perhaps he had never truly seen her as a person. Just as a woman who would give him pleasure.

Richard swallowed. "I will tell no one, I can assure you."

"That does not matter!" She sobbed, tears falling from her eyes. "Because I never want to be married now! Do you not understand, you damned fool? I saw myself married to you, as your wife. That dream is dead now, and you are a liar and thief!"

He looked astonished at her words, but Tabitha did not care anymore. Why should she care for his emotions? He had given little concern to her own, and look where she was now. Despoiled, never to know the touch of a gentleman again because who would touch her after this? It did not matter what he said—the gossips were guessing about their disappearance at the ball together, and nothing could be less scandalous than the truth.

"And you thought I was engaged to another," she said bitterly. "I will never wed."

"I should not have thought that," he said swiftly, trying to reach for her hand. "I apologize, Tabitha–"

"There are quite a few things you should not have said." Tabitha smiled weakly through her tears, moving her hand away from him. "At least I see what sort of a man you are."

She could not say another word. Turning and striding as fast as she could along the path, she allowed the tears to fall freely.

"God blast it all!"

She heard Richard curse under his breath behind her, but she did not turn around. The sound of footsteps echoed in the silence, and once again, a hand reached out and turned her around.

"Look, marriage is not everything," Richard said hastily, "it is not the only thing in life worth doing–"

"'Tis easy for you to say! Yes, it is all very well for a man to say that. You have options, choices before you," she snapped, pulling away from him and walking toward the gate. He followed, keeping up with her. "But for me, the only choice I have–that I ever had–is whether to marry or not, and you have stolen that."

She was walking as quickly as she could. *To be away from him, to escape from the torment of his presence.*

"But surely it is not marriage you should be hoping for but love!"

Tabitha stopped outside the gate and rounded on him, who flinched at the severity of her words. "God's teeth, have you not been listening to a word I have said? You have no idea what love is, what sacrifice is, what devotion and dedication are, so do not think to lecture me on any such subject! And if you dare to come within ten feet of me again, I shall ensure Lieutenant Thomas Perry gives you a sharp lesson in what happens when you disgrace a lady!"

Without waiting to hear his response, she grabbed her skirts and half walked and half ran away from him.

CHAPTER EIGHTEEN

THE ROOM HAD been silent until the bottle, dripping with an amber liquid that was pooling on the floor, slipped from the gentleman's hand and smashed across the floor.

The sound barely made Richard jump. In his right hand was an exquisite whiskey glass. Without concern for the broken glass surrounding him, he brought the glass to his lips, drained it, and placed it on the table. Beside it stood a fresh, unopened bottle.

A log moved in the fire. Richard stared at it hazily, unable to focus on the source of the sound.

Well, this was what drinking gave you. It was difficult to see the attraction his father and brother saw in the habit, but it was impossible to deny it did numb the pain.

Tabitha's bitter words rang in his ears, and he could not erase them from his memory. His throat thickened painfully, and to his horror, a tear fell.

He brushed it away angrily and grabbed at the unopened whiskey bottle.

It took him a few minutes in his hazy state to open the bottle. Richard raised the bottle to pour some more into his empty glass. He would drink himself to death, that would be easier than living in pain.

The door to the study opened and there was an almighty crash. Charlotte, her face absolutely horrified, had dropped her tea tray and all it contained.

"Richard," she breathed.

He waved his glass in welcome. "That is my name."

"And… is that whiskey?" she rushed toward him.

She tried to wrench the glass away out of his hand, but he did not give it up without a struggle.

"No, that's my drink!" he said angrily.

When he eventually let go of the glass, he glared at her.

Charlotte collapsed into the chair opposite him. Before he could say anything, she drank the whiskey herself. "What happened to you?" She placed the empty glass and the bottle she had taken from him on the table behind her chair.

Richard scowled at her, but his expression softened as he chuckled bitterly. "I never thought I would see my sister put a glass of whiskey away like that."

"I never thought I would see my brother drink at all," she retorted. "Where have you been all afternoon? I waited for you at dinner, but I am afraid Cook would not linger beyond seven. I thought you had gone to see Tabitha."

"I did," he said. "Now give me back my–"

"No," she said firmly, an eyebrow raised. "Now tell me exactly what caused you, of all people, to open a bottle of that filthy stuff."

Richard shrugged. "'Tis not bad after the fourth glass."

Charlotte stared at him as though she had never seen him before. "After all these years of avoiding it, of being strong…why have you given up?"

He leaned back in his chair and let his gaze drift toward the fire. "Oh, Charlotte. You have it all wrong. I am not strong, I never have been–I am weak and afraid and alone. Just like father was."

After everything he had done or tried to achieve, he was doomed to repeat the same mistakes. It did not matter what Tabitha said. It did not matter what anyone said.

"You are nothing like our father," Charlotte said coldly, "and he had Mother, though he never cared enough about her to change. Is that you, Richard? Do you care only about yourself? Do you even realize I am right here?"

He shook his head. "It is not that I do not appreciate it, Lotty, but–"

"You paid off the debts, all of them, even when it came at great personal cost," she said fiercely. "Do you not see how different you are to him?"

Guilt, an emotion not in short supply, seared his heart and caused a bitter taste in his mouth that had nothing to do with the whiskey.

"At the cost of your dowry."

He chanced a look at his older sister and saw lines around her eyes he had not noticed before.

Her shoulders slumped but she rallied. "For the good of the family. If you had twenty thousand pounds in your personal fortune, are you honestly telling me you would not have given it up for the family?"

"I am not sure whether I am as noble as you."

"After our idiotic brother drowned his sorrows in a bottle, it was our responsibility to restore the family name," Charlotte said desperately. "And we did!"

"And now it is my turn to drown my sorrows," Richard said with a hiccup. He reached for the whiskey bottle. One more drink, one more bottle, what did it matter? All he wanted to do was remove the distraught look of Tabitha's face from his mind, but there was not enough whiskey in the world to achieve that.

Charlotte slapped his arm away. "Tell me about it, Richard."

"Tell you what?"

She gave him the same scowl she had given him when they were children and she had caught him in a lie.

Richard slumped lower. He could not believe he was discussing his liaisons with Charlotte, but then, who else? It was impossible to hide anything from his sister, and there was no one else he would rather talk to about this.

Well, perhaps one other.

"I have had a…misunderstanding. With Tabitha. Miss Chesworth."

Charlotte raised an eyebrow but said nothing.

A wretched, hot embarrassment overwhelmed him. He felt guilty for what he was about to recount, but there was nothing for it. There was no point in trying to explain the whole, sorry business in part.

"You know me," he said heavily. "My weaknesses and how I have…arrangements with young ladies. They understand what they are getting into, and I never force anyone to do anything they have no wish to."

Charlotte's cheeks reddened slightly, but she nodded.

"I thought I could have such an arrangement with…with Miss Chesworth. But it did not go exactly to plan."

"Exactly?" his sister repeated with a frown. "What are we talking?"

There was no easy way to say it, and he took a deep breath. "I wanted to seduce her, perhaps even make her my mistress if…if we were compatible. I came to like her, and when I made my offer again, she…"

"She got the wrong idea," he said in a rather strangled voice. "Oh God's teeth, Lotty, she thought I was offering marriage and accepted me on those terms. We made love, and the misunderstanding has come to light, and I think I have broken her, Lotty. She is utterly broken."

Silence fell in the study. Why had he not made sure she had understood? Why had he not taken the time explain everything clearly?

His sister reached for the bottle of whiskey, poured herself half a glass, and threw it down her throat.

Richard leaned forward, but she placed the bottle behind her chair once more. "You should not do that, Lotty!"

"*I* should not–what about you?" she burst, glaring at him with such ire that he shrank back into his chair. "My word, Richard, if you are not the most ignorant and irritating fool in all of God's green earth! Are you telling me that you had real happiness in your grasp, the opportunity to be with a woman who likes you–not just admires you, not just interested in your title, but *you*...and you seduced her without any promises for the future?"

Her frustration hit him like a sledgehammer. What could he say? He could not disagree with her, and she saw it in his face. Blowing out her cheeks and shaking her head, she stared in utter disbelief.

"I do not understand you," she said finally. "Help me to understand, Richard. You had something, and you have lost it. How? Why?"

Richard felt the emptiness inside his chest. Tabitha was lost to him. He had not even realized what he had until it was too late.

"It does not matter anyway," he said dully. "Who is to say happiness with her would have kept the temptations at bay? Perhaps..." The thought which had been plaguing him resurfaced. "Perhaps she is better off far away from me."

His sister clicked her tongue in disbelief. "You are the most frightful fool." Yet, there was kindness in her eyes. "We choose our own paths."

Her words were comforting, but it was not the comfort Richard wanted. She could not understand what it was like to be from a long line of terrible men. All the Axwick women had been strong and virtuous.

"I have chosen," he said.

Charlotte snorted. "You have chosen badly. You are choosing misery here, alone in this room, drinking away what you think are your problems, when you have the opportunity to make things right. Why on earth are you not at Miss Chesworth's, explaining everything?"

It all sounded easy. She could not know the complexity of everything with Tabitha; the offer of seduction he had made her, the stolen kisses, the thrill of the chase–and the library, the misunderstanding, the conquest and the sweet release of agonizing delight that had built up for weeks. The confusion, the fear of her betrayal, and the terrible knowledge that it was his stupid fault all the sweetness between them had turned bitter.

His heart was pounding, but it slowed as a new idea crept into his mind. Perhaps it was all incredibly simple.

He cared about her–loved her, even. Was this love, this needing to be with someone no matter what the cost, the desperate need to care for them, hating being apart from them, admiring everything about them, being overwhelmed by the need to rip any other man apart that threatened what he loved?

Something lurched in his stomach.

Oh God, he thought in horror. *I am in love. And alone.*

Marriage suddenly did not seem frightening.

He did love her. Her fire, her spark, the heated passion and wit that he discovered each and every time they had spoken with each other. She was the one bright part of his life. Before he had met her, life was about getting through to the next day, finding money to pay the bills, and keeping the family name alive.

And now? Now he wanted to see her smile. If he spent the rest of his life working to put a smile on Miss Tabitha Chesworth's face, it would surely be a life well lived.

"Charlotte," Richard said slowly, his eyes making their way back to his sister. "I have made a terrible mistake."

She snorted and stood up, taking the whiskey bottle with her. "You are completely right. You have. But mistakes can be fixed. The question is, are you willing to?"

CHAPTER NINETEEN

THE SLIMY EGGS slipped off her fork and onto her plate. Tabitha watched listlessly as her mother's chatter washed over her like a wave onto the shore.

"–and of course, I was not expecting her to be here during this Season, but she told me after her daughter's marriage there was no point staying in London, and here she is! It really is most fortunate, for I did not think we would have any acquaintances also invited to the dinner at the Howards. That makes a rather elegant number for cards afterward, do not you think?"

There was a silence suddenly, and Tabitha saw her smiling expectantly.

"Do not you think?" she repeated.

Tabitha smiled. "I do."

"Ah, I thought you would be pleased! I saw how easy it was for you to converse with her daughter, Adena, and of course, once you befriend the daughter, it is always much easier to speak with the whole family–though of course she is not plain old Adena, but the Marchioness of Dewsbury! Now *that* was a wedding, I am sure you will agree." Her mother paused to gulp some tea and continued. "I cannot wait to see what the marchioness will be wearing this season. Just like I said to dear Mr. Prander…"

The words kept coming, and Tabitha tried to focus on her food, but there was such numbness inside her, she could barely concentrate.

Tabitha, that was about my offer. My offer to seduce you. What I said there, in the library...it was my offer to make love to you. To make both of us happy—to bring both of us pleasure. It was just about that night.

Try as she might, it was impossible to stop hearing those words. Every time she relived the memories of Sydney Gardens, darkness consumed her heart.

After waiting for love for so many years and finding it comical when others had made matches which did not suit them, what had she done?

She had not even found a match. The Duke of Axwick, for that was how she must consider him—had not ever thought of her seriously. He had wanted to ravish her, and now he had moved on.

When she had finally dragged herself to breakfast at ten o'clock, her mother had noted nothing of it and just allowed her daughter, though teary-eyed and silent, to help herself to food.

"You have not eaten anything."

Tabitha's gaze jerked up to see her mother, staring. "No, I have not. I am sorry, Mother."

Her mother frowned. "Are you ill? Should we call out the doctor?"

How could she eat after falling in love with a man who did not exist, and she would be ruined if word ever got out.

Or perhaps it would not matter.

"Tabitha, can you hear me?"

Tabitha jolted, startled from her reverie to see her mother standing with a highly concerned look on her face.

"Please do not concern yourself," Tabitha said with a watery smile. "I am quite well."

She was evidently not convincing, however.

"Keytes," Mrs. Chesworth called, and their butler appeared. "Keytes, please be so good as to send a quick note around to Doctor—"

"Please, I am quite well," Tabitha interrupted, forcing more feeling into her words. "I am tired, that is all. I...I slept badly."

To prove there was nothing to worry about, she picked up her fork and stuffed some cured ham into her mouth. It was dry. She tried not to gag as nausea overwhelmed her.

The butler glanced between mother and daughter. Tabitha chewed the ham with difficulty.

"Hmm." Mrs. Chesworth sat and waved Keytes away with a hand. "We will see how you fare this afternoon."

Bowing, the butler left the breakfast room. Tabitha chose a piece of toast and carefully buttered it, wincing at the noise of the scraping knife.

"May I ask," said her mother quietly as she poured herself another cup of tea, "whether these thoughts keeping you up at night are about a certain handsome someone who shall remain nameless between us? Is he likely to call again today?"

Tabitha flushed. The duke was not going to call today or any other day in the future. She would never see him again, and when she had thought about all the things she had wanted to say to him, she had cried endlessly.

How could she have ever thought of giving herself to him? Had she valued herself so little?

"–I said, are you?"

Tabitha heard the slam of a teacup back on the table and saw her mother staring at her with a hint of annoyance.

"I am sorry, what did you say?"

For the first time in their conversation, Mrs. Chesworth glared with definite irritation. "Tabitha, I have the strangest impression you are not listening to me."

Tabitha sighed. "My apologies again, Mother, I…I am very tired. Please, would you repeat what you said?"

"I said, I am going to the Pump Room in twenty minutes," her mother repeated, "and if you would like to accompany me, then you are going to have to be quick."

The thought of leaving the house and going into public was too much.

"I think I would rather stay at home today," she said finally. "I have a slight headache coming, and I think it best I remain here."

Mrs. Chesworth looked critically at her daughter and hummed under her breath. Then she threw up her hands and smiled. "You are your own person, Tabitha, and it is not for me to tell you what to do. Stay here. Rest–your letter should be a nice way to spend an hour or two."

Tabitha blinked. "Letter?"

Mrs. Chesworth laughed as she rose from her seat. "Really, Tabitha, you must not have slept at all last night! The letter Keytes gave you ten minutes ago, my dear, it is right beside your plate."

Without another word, she bustled out of the room.

Tabitha looked down. Beside her plate, just as her mother had said, was a letter. It looked as though it had travelled a long way with a slight rip in one corner and what could be a water stain across one side. Someone must have had placed their glass upon it at one point in its travels, but the handwriting was still clear, and she recognized it.

Mabel. A smile crept over her face. A letter from Mabel–of course, she had promised she would write as soon as she was able, and it had been weeks since they had last seen each other, weeks since...the wedding.

Swallowing the painful thought of weddings and marriage, Tabitha picked up the letter and used her clean knife to break the seal. It was not nearly as long as she had hoped for.

Dear Tabitha,

As I write you these lines, it is strange indeed to think how long it has been since we saw each other–almost five weeks! Five long weeks.

So much changed on that day, and of course so much has happened since then, the lieutenant has just reminded me of how much we have seen! Paris, of course, where we spent some lovely time with his cousin who is still serving out there. The gentlemen of our army are, without a doubt, some of the finest young men I have ever seen, Tabitha, and I have to say, I consider myself very fortunate indeed to have married one.

The food in France is not at all what you would think, and I do not recommend it. Darling Perry was brave enough to try snails, but I shrieked that I could not. The darling man did not force me.

After Paris was Lyon, which is farther than I could have dreamed. After that, Marseilles…or to tell the truth, it could have been the other way around, these French cities all start to merge into one. But when we reached Italy, that was when I truly fell in love with traveling.

Oh, Tabitha, if I could show you some of the marvels I have seen! I truly do not think I will ever find true comfort at home after traveling so far. It is like stepping into a history book, being here in Rome where we have been these last three days, and although we are due to leave here in one more day, I have begged Perry whether we may not stay a full week, for there is much more to see. I feel one cannot spend too much time in Rome.

It was in Rome that I answered for the first time to Mrs. Perry, and I cannot tell you what a joy it was. You spend so much of your life answering to one name that it is a shock to suddenly have another.

And it feels right. I feel I have been Mrs. Perry for hundreds of years, and I would not change it for the world. As I think back to our wedding day (and that does feel like hundreds of years ago!) I am grateful I had you by my side as I blossomed from plain old Miss Reed to Mrs. Thomas Perry.

Tell me all your news, if you have any.

With love from your dearest cousin,
Mabel

She carefully folded the letter and smiled. Mabel's absence from Bath had never been more keenly felt, and she could have benefited greatly from a friend's listening ear now. There was no mention of her own letter, no questions about the gentleman who had stolen her heart. But Mabel's mind was absolutely swimming with married life. It was strange to think of her as Mrs. Perry.

So much changed on that day, and of course so much as happened since then...

Mabel could not know how right she was. So much had occurred since they had last seen each other.

In a wild moment of madness, Tabitha's mind was overwhelmed with the image of herself walking down the aisle in a blue wedding gown, with no one else in the church except the Reverend Michaels and Richard St. Maur, waiting for her at the altar.

But then he, too, disappeared, and she was left in the church to face the reverend alone and abandoned.

She swallowed. But what if the story was different? What if it had all been different? What if instead they could be happy and in love, wedded with nothing to keep them apart from each other? She saw them sitting happily in the library, the same library where she thought he had proposed to her–and a child ran into the room, a young boy with the same hair as her but with Richard's wicked laugh.

A tear fell. Tabitha brushed it from the letter, unfolded the paper, and read it again.

She had expected to feel envious once she received news of her cousin, but she was not.

A wedding was all very well, and it was undoubtedly nice to be the most important person in the room for a day–but it was just one day. It was a marriage that she wanted, a real one, in which she was not just loved but respected.

That was what Mabel had found. Lieutenant Perry clearly adored his wife, and that did spark envy.

Another tear fell and smudged a line of writing on the paper. Tabitha folded it up as she dashed away her tears and picked up that morning's newspaper. Rifling through the pages to the gossip where she could at least escape into someone else's life.

A small paragraph caught her eye.

We are pleased to discover that one of the most noble of our dear town's current inhabitants, a certain duke, has finally left bankruptcy behind and become solvent again. After years of struggling to pay a single bill, it is our delight to report that he now has money to burn–and is likely to use it to pave the route down the aisle with a certain young lady who has journeyed down it before not once, not twice, but thrice–but with no personal happy outcome.

This was another guess off the mark, surely. The *Bath Chronicle* always suggested wild things and before, they had always made her smile.

Could Richard be so mercenary? Had that been his true purpose, to bed her and then trick her out of her fortune?

Surely their encounters had been more. In every encounter with him, he had always made her happy. Sometimes she did not understand him or herself when she was with him, but he had made her happy.

He had never asked about her money. Her fortune had never been a topic of conversation for them. But now that she came to think about it, it was surely not possible he had sought her only for her body alone.

Without warning, she stood up, the newspaper falling to the floor. What was she doing here, lounging around and wallowing in her misery–when she could try to be happy?

He cared about her in some way, though what way, she was not sure, but he did. He made her feel things she had never experienced before.

He still wanted her, and what did it matter if it was not for marriage? Tabitha swallowed, but continued thinking. Who cared what society thought if joy could be within her grasp?

She almost laughed aloud. It was ridiculous, but it made sense. As long as he was honest with her from this day onward, could they perhaps reach a new understanding?

A slight tug of regret pulled at her heart, but she pushed it away.

No, this was the way it had to be–the only way she could find happiness again. Marriage was all very well, but true happiness was not always found there. She would be with Richard as his mistress. Nothing could replace how he made her feel.

She wanted him.

Tabitha walked to the door but was intercepted by her mother.

"Ah, Tabitha! You are coming to the Pump Room, then?"

Tabitha stared. "Pump Room? No, I am sorry, Mother. I am actually in a hurry to go and see–"

"I would not bother," Mrs. Chesworth said breezily, returning to the hallway and pulling on a pair of black leather gloves. "I have just heard from the butler no less–the St. Maurs have decided to leave Bath and go back to the family estate. They left this morning, in quite a rush, Keytes says."

Tabitha deflated, her shoulders slumping. From such hope to such misery. He had retreated, leaving her behind.

"It must be very difficult for his lordship to be back there," tutted her mother, adjusting her bonnet in the looking glass.

Tabitha snorted. "Honestly, Mother, how difficult can it be for a duke to return to his home?"

Bonnet still crooked and with a rather menacing hatpin in her hand, Mrs. Chesworth turned to stare at her daughter in frank amazement. "You mean…you mean to tell me you do not know?"

Tabitha frowned. "Know?"

Her mother hesitated. "I thought you had heard, my dear, otherwise, I would not have…well, I suppose there is no harm in telling you, such a close friend of the duke's as you are…"

She simply stared at her mother in confusion.

"It was all over town when it happened, but of course you were very young then. His father had a terrible reputation."

Tabitha took a step forward and removed the hatpin from her mother's hand. "I know about all that," she said quietly, carefully moving her mother's bonnet to rest at an elegant angle.

"But what you were probably unaware of," Mrs. Chesworth said, catching her daughter's eye in the looking glass, "was that he used to beat his sons. Terribly so, I heard from Doctor Wade. There was talk the daughter–Charlotte, I think, or Caroline–was beaten, too."

Tabitha stared in horror at her mother's reflection. "No," she breathed.

He surely could not have suffered in such an awful way–and Lady Charlotte as well? How could Richard never have mentioned this to her?

Her mother tutted, and Tabitha carefully slid the hatpin into place.

"'Tis no wonder the current duke has taken so long to settle down," said Mrs. Chesworth sadly, turning to face her daughter with a wry smile, "with a father like that."

Tabitha nodded mutely.

"Now," her mother said briskly. "I will be home for luncheon, I expect, and I presume I will see you here then? If your headache does not become anything worse, I mean?"

Tabitha swallowed. There was so much about Richard she had not discovered. This small revelation proved that. She could now see the lingering effects of that damage in him. There were scars there, and it would take time for them to heal.

She wanted to be with him. She loved him, and whether or not Richard wanted to marry her, she needed to be with him.

"No," she said, and found to her surprise her voice was calm. "I am sorry, Mother, but I am leaving town."

Mrs. Chesworth had already started walking toward the door, but she paused in surprise and looked back. "Really? For how long?"

Tabitha smiled. "I think I am about to find out."

CHAPTER TWENTY

RICHARD THREW DOWN the book he had attempted to read for the last twenty minutes. He had grabbed a few volumes from the library in Bath, the one at Stonehaven Lacey left so sparse after the sale of its contents, but he had not taken in a single word.

Ye gods, was there anything worse than returning to this place? Every time he thought he was free from it, he was pulled right back. Back to the home filled with secrets and pain.

If only Charlotte had accompanied him. She had almost been convinced, but just the day before had agreed to act as chaperone for Miss Darby, and that meant staying in Bath for the next week. It was only when Charlotte was not with him that he realized how he depended on her. He had left Bath four days ago, but it felt like four hundred years.

And there they are, your true colors. I knew they would come out eventually, and your true intentions, your true interest would be revealed. All you wanted was my body.

Richard sighed and got to his feet, glass in hand. Like a caged animal, he began to pace the room, shaking his head as though that would rid his mind of her words. They pained him more than anything, and the more he dwelled on them...well, it was impossible to deny their truth.

He winced. It was still painful to think of her, why?

He stopped at the high windows overlooking the lawn. It had been foolish of him to mention the other women he had previously encountered. Why had he done so? He had been selfish there, selfish and stupid. He had feared losing her and had lashed out when really…

Richard moved to the fireplace and stopped pacing. His mother had placed a looking glass there to bring light into the overly dark room. The whiskey glass was empty now, the liquid scattered over the carpet. He put it on the mantle and gazed at himself in the looking glass.

Red-rimmed eyes looked back. There were new wrinkles and a rather wan tinge to his complexion. Worse of all was the sense of absolute desolation in his eyes. He looked lost. Completely lost.

Richard's gaze dropped to his feet. He had been handsome all his adult life and the ladies of the *ton* had flocked to him, but his fine features had not helped him when real love faced him.

Real love. He had not believed such a thing existed a year ago, and now look at him!

No, he could not think of her like that, it did her no justice. He cared about her in a way he had never cared before. His sister had always spoken of soulmates, and he had laughed at her, but now… he was not sure.

What else could explain this ache inside his chest, as though his heart had been scooped out and taken away? He felt empty without her. It was an ache not only in his loins, but his stomach, his chest, and his mind. An ache nothing could cure.

How long he stood staring into the looking glass waiting for the reflected Richard St. Maur to give some sort of answer, he did not know. He would have remained there indefinitely if the door to the hallway had not opened, and Matthews stepped in.

"I do beg your pardon, your grace," said the butler smoothly. "I hate to disturb you, but there is a young lady to see you."

Richard snorted, and he saw Matthews raise an eyebrow.

"I speak nothing but the truth, your grace," he said in a reproving voice Richard would not have accepted from any other servant. "She is waiting in the hallway. Shall I send her in?"

The duke hung his head, rattling through the extensive list of eligible young ladies who lived in the local village who threw themselves at him whenever he was back. Most of them had no wish to come here, sent by their mamas in the hope of catching him–Maria Holland perhaps, or Rebecca Sutton?

"Whoever it is, send them away," he said with a growl. "I have no wish to see anyone today, blast you."

Despite the incivility, Matthews replied calmly. "If I were to be so bold as to give advice to your grace, I would recommend you see her."

"I did not ask for your opinion," snapped Richard, jerking his head around to glare at the servant.

Matthews met his irritable stare with a perfectly calm one of his own, not moving an inch.

Richard sighed. "Unless it is Miss Tabitha Chesworth, Matthews, send them away and go to hell yourself."

"Now, that is not a very nice way to speak to such a kind man, is it Matthews?"

It was a woman's voice, and she pushed past the butler and glared at Richard, whose mouth fell open.

It was Tabitha.

Nothing coherent came to Richard's mind, and he could say nothing to the mirage standing before him. He had wished for her to be here, and here she was. It was a trick of the whiskey.

"Why thank you very much, Miss Chesworth," said Matthews smoothly with a bow of the head.

"You are very welcome," said Tabitha, ignoring Richard but beaming at the older gentleman as she pulled off her gloves and unpinned her bonnet. "That will be all, Matthews."

Richard stared as the butler took the proffered hat and gloves, inclined his head once again to the young woman, and left the room, a smile on his face as he closed the door behind him.

"Y-you cannot speak to my servants like that!" Richard managed to bluster.

He did not know whether he wanted Tabitha to shout, laugh, or speak coldly–all of those options and more spun through his mind, and he could not tell which was worse.

She did none of them. Completely ignoring his words, she strode toward him. For one heady heartbeat, Richard was convinced she was going to kiss him. He almost reached out for her, her softness and her warmth, everything that was Tabitha.

She reached for the whiskey bottle and poured the amber liquid into the fireplace, tutting. Without meeting his eyes, she walked away from him and placed the bottle on a table.

It was only then that she raised her gaze to his and said fiercely, "No husband of mine is going to drink like that. Four o'clock in the afternoon! Shame on you."

If he had not been leaning against the mantlepiece, Richard would have fallen over. Tabitha, *Tabitha* at Stonehaven Lacey? Ordering around his servants, and them letting her, and what's more, ordering him!

This was not the reunion he had expected. Richard felt his chest grow warm with outrage.

"T-Tabitha," he spluttered, with no thought how to continue, but certain he had to say something. This was his chance to make things right, and he had no idea how. It was easy to kiss away most differences, but this time, charm was not the answer.

Before he could say another word, she smiled and stood a mere foot from him. She took a deep breath. "You do know I love you, don't you?"

He stopped searching for the right words as his gaze raked over her face. She looked fearful, hopeful, angry, and desperately happy. How could so many emotions be in just one expression?

By God, she was so precious. Was there any chance he was still lying on the sofa, in a drunken stupor, dreaming?

"'Tis strange, but I have never loved anyone like this," Tabitha continued softly. "I truly think I love you more than I could ever imagine caring for anyone else."

Something painful stabbed through Richard's heart. He wanted to reach out for her, but she was a thousand leagues away.

"And so," she took a deep breath, "I have seen Mr. Birch the accountant, and that is that."

She stared in silence, a smile playing on her face, but Richard had no idea what she meant.

"That is that?" he muttered.

She nodded. "I gave it some serious thought, because–well, it is quite a step. But I thought it was for the best, and Mr. Birch agreed, and so...well, 'tis done."

Her smile brightened, but Richard was still confused. "Tabitha– Miss Chesworth, I have absolutely no idea what you are talking about. What has happened? What have you done?"

She laughed gently. "Why, I have gifted you my entire fortune, Richard."

He stumbled over the fender and had to grasp the mantlepiece to stop from falling to the floor. Her dowry–her *entire* fortune, made over to him?

Tabitha laughed and reached out to take his hand. She was real, definitely not the product of a whiskey stupor, and she squeezed his hand with such warmth, that he smiled weakly.

"Oh, Richard, money is such nonsense," she said quietly, her green eyes never leaving him. "It has hurt you for the lack of it, and it has weighed on me ever since hearing that disgusting Mr. Lister speak of my dowry in more glowing terms than myself. What joy has money? I have fixed the problem. Now neither of us need worry."

"You...you are mad," said Richard finally, a smile turning up the corners of his mouth as he beheld the beautiful woman he loved. "I did not want your money, Tabitha, and I utterly refuse to accept it!"

She was still smiling. "I am afraid it does not work like that. I have talked it all through with Mr. Birch, and he is quite the expert, and well–the transfer has been made."

Richard laughed, shaking his head at the nonsense of it, but did not let go of Tabitha's hand. He wanted her so badly, he could sweep everything off the table and have her right there, but he wanted more. More than an encounter. More than her body.

He wanted her. In some strange twist of fate, he did not quite understand, she was here. He was not going to let this opportunity slip through his fingers.

"There is always a way," he said gently, pulling on her hand so she was forced to either let go or take a small step toward him. "It cannot be impossible to return the money, Miss Chesworth–and that is what I intend to do."

She did not ask him to call her Tabitha, and he felt panic spark up his spine. Could it be possible she loved him, but did not want him?

"Return the money? What nonsense," she said. "I will repeat the transaction again, and there we will go, around in circles. I do think that is a little wasteful for Mr. Birch's time, do you not agree?"

Richard could not help himself, he laughed. He pulled her into his arms, and she came willingly. She was his Tabitha, the only woman worth anything in the world, the only woman he ever wanted in his arms again.

"Even I," he said eventually, tilting her head so he could gaze into her face, "could not have made this up. By God, Tabitha, you are here–and you love me. I have never thought love was even possible. I had shied away from any thought of it, but you have shown me love is not always something you choose. I may have picked you out at a wedding, but you have had the greater hold on me from that moment, and I-I would do anything for you, because you are the most precious–"

"The whole world thought you were courting me for my money," Tabitha said softly, smiling as she interrupted him. "I thought you were courting me because of my beauty–"

"And your body," growled Richard with a smile, moving his hands to her slender waist and trying not to groan aloud.

"And my body," she repeated with a smile. "But really, what were you courting me for?"

Silence fell between them. She looked at him, searching for the truth. Richard swallowed. He had to tell her, though it would sound ridiculous at first.

"I courted you at first for your body," he said with a slightly shameful smile, "and then your wit, and then your company. But by the end, I wanted your soul—to love you completely."

Her mouth opened in surprise. And then they were kissing as if they never had before.

Richard's hand was on her cheek, guiding her lips to his own, and she welcomed it. She moaned as his hands moved to her waist, pulling her closer. He shivered as her wandering hands found his buttocks and clasped them, hesitantly but then with greater certainty.

They clung to each other, the passion and misunderstandings of the last few days pouring out in uncontrolled desire.

Eventually, they broke apart.

"I love you," Richard muttered, his forehead against hers, arms tightly around her. "I love you, Tabitha, and I will go on loving you come what may."

"Why has it taken you so long to say that?" she asked.

"Because I am an idiot."

Tabitha laughed. "Yes, you are, but you are going to need to change. No child of mine is going to have an idiot for a father."

Richard did not mishear the words.

Mouth open, he staggered a few steps away so he could see her properly, all of her. She was joyful—radiant. He raised his eyebrows in a silent question, and she nodded.

"Yes," she whispered. "I am sure."

CHAPTER TWENTY-ONE

"**Y**OU MEAN?" WORDS failed him, and Tabitha tried to stem her giggles as happiness overwhelmed her. It did her soul good to see him this confused, excited, happy, and with a pinch of fear in there for good measure.

She nodded as she calmed herself. After all, the father of her child deserved an explanation.

"As sure as I can be. I missed my menses...ten days ago? It has never happened before," she said, her gaze lowered in embarrassment. "I have spoken with no fewer than three doctors, all in utter confidence you understand, and they agree I am with child."

Her hands moved unconsciously to her stomach where beneath her gown, a new life was starting.

She had expected shock, she had expected surprise, but this complete lack of expression from Richard...it frightened her. He had stepped to the other side of the room, head in his hands. Was he going to abandon her, even after admitting they cared so dearly for each other, now that he knew there was a child?

In a swift movement that made her gasp, he strode across the room and pulled her into his arms, kissing her with a new reverence. She responded warmly, wrapping her arms around him.

Hope and fear danced in his brown eyes. "Are you quite sure?"

She laughed. "'Tis impossible to be completely sure until a few weeks have passed, but...yes. I feel different, different in a way I do not think I can explain in words. I can barely keep my breakfast down, for one thing!"

He laughed and poured kisses onto her cheeks, eyes, mouth, until she pulled away.

"Which I hope you realize means you will have to marry me," she said with a playful, stern look. "I cannot have the future seventeenth Duke of Axwick unable to claim his birthright because his parents were not married."

"Well, you have heard the phrase," Richard said with a teasing smile. "Three times a bridesmaid, never a bride. I think the odds may be against you."

She tapped him lightly on the nose. "Is that any way to speak to a woman with child? And even if we are not," she said, "I am sure we can try again."

He growled and pulled her tightly to him. "I am going to make absolutely sure."

Tabitha grinned. "You will have plenty of time for all that after we are married."

"And soon," Richard grinned, lowering his lips to hers.

Tabitha reveled in the kiss, the closeness, the safety, and passion restrained but not for long. He was hers and she was his, and nothing could break them apart, nothing.

"Wait a moment. You have transferred your entire–your entire fortune! Tabitha, that is thirty thousand pounds."

She looked up without speaking. He had been wild and untamed when she had met him, only interested in bedding her and taking his pleasure. Now he worshipped the ground she walked on, without thought of himself. Until now.

"It is."

Something like horror flickered across his face. "Tabitha, 'tis a fortune!"

"And is mine to give," she said, kissing him swiftly. "Do you think I have not considered this, that I have thoughtlessly made such a decision? But I am yours, Richard, it will amount to the same thing once we are married. And what care have we for money?"

"Only those with money say that," he muttered with a grin.

She tapped him on the nose again. "You are a duke and can hardly talk–and now your fortunes are restored. I am just happy that I could be a part of it."

He stared, unblinking, for what felt like a very long time. Surely, he was not going to try to argue with her again?

And then Richard smiled. "Fortunes restored? You could have come to me penniless, and I would have been the richest man in the world. You have given me yourself, unreservedly, and perhaps a child, too? I do not think there is any bridesmaid in the world that deserves her own happy ending more than you."

EPILOGUE

TABITHA COULD FEEL her breath rising from her lungs and tried to focus on the way it disappeared in the cool spring air. It was just a day. Just another day. She watched the light fall through the stained-glass windows. With one shaking hand, she smoothed her pale, blue gown and clung onto a small poesy of flowers–this time, her favorites. White roses and red poked through the greenery she had picked herself that morning. She would not drop them, no matter how quickly her heart fluttered.

Organ music rang out in the quiet air, breaking the silence around her. As she clutched the flowers tightly, she could feel a heavy signet ring on the third finger of her right hand. It was cold but warmed her in a way nothing else could.

"Are you ready?"

Her mother smiled, and Tabitha returned the gesture. She had guided her through so much and would now take her the last few steps toward a future she wanted desperately–but could not imagine being given.

Tabitha nodded. She cleared her throat and took a step forward.

It was impossible not to be overwhelmed with happiness as she stepped slowly but surely down the long aisle. Tears pinched at the corners of her eyes, and she quashed the emotion for fear of completely losing control.

This was it. This was her moment. She could never have imagined such a day, though she had wished for it more than she would ever confess.

Every person in St. Gabriel's turned slowly to look at her and smiled, and this time, unlike the three times before, they did not then look past her to see another. This time, their gazes followed her with each step, because at this wedding, unlike all those before, it was she, Miss Tabitha Chesworth, who was the bride.

It took her an age to reach the front of the church, but she kept her attention on the gentleman whose silhouette she could just make out.

Richard. Richard St. Maur, sixteenth Duke of Axwick. He was staring as though he had never seen a woman before.

"And how," he whispered in such a low voice that even the Reverend Michaels could not hear him, "did you ever manage to force me into this?"

A smile danced across his face, and Tabitha laughed, forced to quell the noise as the vicar glared sternly at them, then smiled beneficently at his congregation.

"Dearly beloved, welcome on this brisk and bright spring day. We are gathered here today…"

Tabitha was overwhelmed as the familiar words echoed through the church, but not so overcome to ignore her future husband's words.

"I had to," she whispered back with a grin. "You stole all my money, and this was the only way I could think of to get it back!"

Richard grinned, and Tabitha stared, greedily taking in the sight of him—the hint of strength, the controlled but powerful movement of his arms.

"Nay, you are the thief," he murmured with a smile. "You are the one who stole my heart."

Tabitha giggled as her mouth fell open in mock horror, but before she could respond, the rings were brought forward. She turned to hand her poesy bouquet to Charlotte who was her bridesmaid.

Charlotte stepped forward and halted her gentle crying into a lace handkerchief.

"...forever hold thy peace," concluded Reverend Michaels, glancing out across the church for anyone to object. When silence echoed for at least fifty heartbeats, if Tabitha was any judge, he smiled and continued. "Wilt thou have this woman to thy wedded wife, to live together after God's ordinance in the holy estate of matrimony? Wilt thou love her, comfort her, honor, and keep her, in sickness and in health; and, forsaking all others, keep thee only unto her, so long as ye both shall live?"

He was waiting for Richard, and Tabitha followed his gaze, her heart in her throat. This was the time when he gave himself to her, gave up the idea of bachelorhood, and promised to be with her forever.

She watched with growing concern as he said not a word. His eyes were on the reverend, and he seemed unable to utter a sound. Surely, he would not do this to her? He would not leave her unwed and shamed and with child at the altar?

Without thinking, Tabitha reached out and took his hand. It was sweaty and warm. The sensation made him look at her, and as soon as their gazes met, all the tension in his shoulders and jaw disappeared. His dark eyes lost their fear, and he squeezed her hand tightly.

"I will." The words were said in a strong voice, and Tabitha relaxed.

The rest of the ceremony disappeared in a blur, and it was only when Reverend Michaels's words, "I pronounce that they be man and wife together," reached her ears, that she realized it had happened.

They were married.

In a whirlwind of congratulations, joy, excitement, and stolen kisses, Tabitha found herself standing on the lawn at Stonehaven Lacey with her hand in her husband's and feet dancing in the clouds.

Well-wishers surrounded them, but one broke from the crowd and came to hug her.

"I could not be more pleased to be proved wrong," laughed Charlotte as she clasped her new sister closely. "It is clear to anyone who loves Richard that he is absolutely besotted with you."

Tabitha laughed as Charlotte pulled away. "I do not think I could have asked for a better husband, nor a better welcome into a family. Thank you for being my bridesmaid, Charlotte. I do not think I would have had the courage to marry today without you."

She laughed, and Tabitha sensed bitterness beneath it. "Well, it certainly beats being a chaperone any day."

Before Tabitha could ask her what she meant, a young lady she recognized as Miss Mary Darby approached them with a smile.

"Lady Charlotte? I beg a moment of your time and apologize for the intrusion, your grace."

Tabitha blinked, wondering who Miss Darby could be apologizing to, but before she could ask, Charlotte gave a brittle smile and said, "Yes, Miss Darby?"

The young lady smiled nervously and continued, "'Tis only that I thought you may be attending *The Magic Flute* in Bath next week, and I would very much like to attend also, but my father is too unwell to leave the house, and I have been asked to attend by William Lennox– the Duke of Richmond. Of course, I may not attend alone, so I was wondering whether you would accompany me and act as chaperone?"

Tabitha glanced at her sister-in-law and saw the pain Miss Darby unwittingly caused. To be asked to act as a chaperone, as though one was truly past the age of love and marriage, …it was not well done of Miss Darby. She did not blame Charlotte for hesitating at such a scandalously thoughtless request.

But her elder was evidently a better woman than she, for Charlotte nodded. "Of course, Miss Darby. I would be delighted to accompany you. Please send round the details in a notecard, so I shall ensure not to engage myself for anything else that evening."

Miss Darby was nothing but raptures, and Charlotte squeezed Tabitha's hand gently before walking away with the excitable young woman.

Tabitha sighed and shook her head. Before she could think how to rescue Charlotte from such a fate, she felt Richard's strong arms come around her waist.

"And how is the Duchess of Axwick feeling?" he murmured in her ear.

Tabitha looked out at the throng of guests who were laughing and talking on the lawn of Stonehaven Lacey, and it was only Richard's soft laughter that nudged her memory.

"I am not sure if I will ever become accustomed to hearing myself described as the Duchess of Axwick! How does anyone learn to–"

But she was interrupted by her mother's voice. "Yes, I am the mother of the bride–the Duchess of Axwick, that is, of course, what I must call her now. Yes, I am very proud..."

Richard chuckled and released her from his grasp as Tabitha rolled her eyes. "Honestly, I do wish she were not quite so ridiculous."

"Everyone is a little ridiculous," he countered, leading her by the hand into the house through the large French doors in the drawing room, and inclining his head at even more guests who filled each room. "Even you."

Tabitha arched an eyebrow as they meandered from one room into another. "Me? I think not. What do you–oh!"

Without any warning, Richard pulled her through a door into the servant's corridor and shut it behind him, silencing the noise of their guests.

"What the–"

"Shh!" Richard placed a hand on his lips and leaned against the door with his ear, listening closely. What could he be thinking?

Her curiosity got the better of her, and she stepped forward to lean against the door. "What are you listening for?"

In a swift movement and with a dark smile, he pushed her so she fell against the door and crushed her lips with his own.

Laughing through the kiss, Tabitha batted him away and glared with a mocking air. "Ah, so that is your game, is it?"

"Of course it is," he growled with a devilish spark in his grin. "Do I have any other?"

She did not reply in words, but pulled him up the stairs to the servants' bedroom. He knew exactly where she was leading him, to the same sort of place where they had first made love. It was just as sparse, but as she closed the door behind them and leaned against it, she smiled wickedly.

Richard groaned and rushed toward her. His lips possessed her, teasing her with the temptation of greater pleasure until she moaned, and he gifted her by ravishing her mouth with his tongue.

"I have been longing to do this all day," she muttered as he kissed her neck.

His hands had moved from her waist and pushed at her skirts, holding them up to reveal that special place of hers. With a hungry look in his eyes, he asked, "Do you think we can be quiet enough to make love against this door without anyone finding us?"

A spark of excitement rushed through Tabitha as she looked at the man she loved. Then she smiled at her husband. "I am always willing to find out."

His next kiss overwhelmed her, but it was nothing to his words. "Never a bridesmaid again, you delicious duchess. I think I may have an addictive soul after all."

She pulled away, her heart pounding, yearning for his touch. "You do? Why, what do you think you have an addiction to?"

He smiled. She fell in love with him all over again as he fumbled with the buttons on his breeches, freeing himself and thrusting inside her, making her gasp with pleasure. "You, of course."

Wondering whether Lady Charlotte, the eternal chaperone will ever find her happily ever after? Find out now in Always the Chaperone.

Make sure you grab the rest of the series to follow the stories of many of the other characters of this book, including Miss Emma Tilbury, Lady Letitia Cavendish, Miss Priscilla Seton, Miss Theodosia Ashbrooke, and Miss Sophia Worsley.

Please do leave a review if you have enjoyed this book–I love reading your thoughts, comments, and even critiques!

You can also receive my news, special offers, and updates by signing up to my mailing list at www.subscribepage.com/emilymurdoch.

About Emily E K Murdoch

If you love falling in love, then you've come to the right place.

I am a historian and writer and have a varied career to date: from examining medieval manuscripts to designing museum exhibitions, to working as a researcher for the BBC to working for the National Trust.

My books range from England 1050 to Texas 1848, and I can't wait for you to fall in love with my heroes and heroines!

Follow me on twitter and instagram @emilyekmurdoch, find me on facebook at facebook.com/theemilyekmurdoch, and read my blog at www.emilyekmurdoch.com.

Made in the USA
Coppell, TX
12 May 2020

24910888R00095